Three Tales woven together by a handsome youth, a beautiful valley, and hard, towering columns.

Buck Private is the story of strapping Wyoming lad Buck Hartigan, who enlists in the Army, where he discovers his true nature. Peter has hinted that Buck is his ideal mate, perhaps his ideal self. Buck's proportions are enticing but not overbearing, which Peter often yearned for in himself and a mate.

The Anaconda Copper tells the tale of a Montana Sheriff whose legendary member earned him the nickname "Stack" in honor of the giant smokestack that looms over the town. Stack meets Buck, who is on his way to a ranch in the Big Hole River Valley but finds his perfect mate in a man he'd often admired but never knew was like him.

Bunkhouse Buddies has the honor of being Peter Schutes's first novel, penned in the late 1950s while living on a ranch in Montana. Buck arrives at the Cock's Crow Ranch, where he discovers he is not the only big boy who enjoys the pleasures of gay sex.

BIG HOLE RIVER

Rugged Tales of the Wild West

PETER SCHUTES

Big Hole River
Copyright © 2023 by Peter Schutes Publishing.
First Pulp Edition © 2024
All Rights Reserved.

ISBN: 978-1-963667-06-6

No part of this publication may be reproduced, distributed, or transmitted in any form or by any means, including photocopying, recording, or other electronic or mechanical methods, without the publisher's prior written permission, except as permitted by U.S. copyright law.

The story, all names, characters, and incidents portrayed in this production are fictitious. No identification with actual persons (living or deceased), places, buildings, and products is intended or should be inferred.

Cover Illustration by Kate Woods-Chisholm

This book is for ADULT AUDIENCES ONLY. It contains substantial sexually explicit scenes with multiple partners and graphic language which may be considered offensive by some readers.

All sexual activity in this work is consensual, and all sexually active characters are 18 years of age or older.

CONTENTS

FOREWORD FROM THE PUBLISHER

Two threads run through this book that tie all three stories together. All three feature Buck Hartigan, the well-endowed blond cherub who lives to serve. They also connect through the titular Big Hole River. This rural part of Montana is where Buck ultimately ends up living in a bunkhouse on a horse ranch.

The thread that ties all of Peter Schutes's stories together is size. Cock size. Big, small, enormous, tiny, or just average, the cock is the center of all of Peter's fiction, just as his cock was the inescapable center of his life.

Peter wrote the *Big Hole River* series in reverse chronological order. *Bunkhouse Buddies* takes place last, but it was the first erotica book Peter ever wrote. He created Buck, an idealized version of himself. Buck was really big, but not crushingly huge like Peter. His carefree attitude and easy sexuality were traits that Peter tried to engender in himself but often failed.

We see Peter's less-than-ideal self in several of the characters. Sergeant Dixon is a morally corrupt version of Peter. Sheriff Dowd and Lars Johnsson are an impossible couple, as Peter says in his Afterword. Sal and Bear are two more facets of Peter, each cripplingly large and lonely for companionship and sex.

When you read *The Autobiography of Peter Schutes*, you discover his love for men with little penises. They, too, appear in these stories.

The New Yorker Vinnie makes up for his small endowment with his muscles, particularly his thick forearm! Mayfield Paine has a tiny penis, too. The Sheriff likens it to a large clitoris. Like Peter, he gets off fucking men who have little choice but to submit to passive anal sex. Buck enjoys dominating Mike, the top dog at Cock's Crow Ranch, whose less-than-average endowment creates a Napoleon complex.

We hope you will enjoy these rugged stories of the Great Plains and the West.

I

BUCK PRIVATE

INTRODUCTION BY THE AUTHOR

I created Buck Hartigan in the early 1960s on a Smith-Corona manual typewriter whose keys were so sticky that I nearly broke a finger every time I used the letter *z*. He makes an appearance in a later book of mine, *The Anaconda Copper*, and so I felt compelled to write his back story. He learned the joys of gay sex before he joined the army. His impressive cock was a perfect tool in every way.

Buck was one of my favorite characters. He had many things I lacked, and where I had too much, he had just a little more than needed. Many of my characters come from real encounters in my life. Buck is pure fiction - a beautiful creation that sprung fully formed from my temple.

I hope that reading this serves as an instruction manual for the repressed homosexual, teaching him the joys and liberties of the flesh. Be carefree, young reader, for Freedom is our birthright. Have sex with other men; taste the pleasures that our creator gave us and expects us to enjoy!

BREAKING IN BUCK

Buck Hartigan was popular with the girls at Cheyenne High. He had a cherubic face, long lashes, blue eyes, and curly blond locks. His average frame was thick but not chunky. He had plenty of muscle and a nice, round butt. He probably caught the eyes of a few boys, but he didn't notice. He wasn't into that sort of thing. Big titties and tight pussies were his kryptonite.

It didn't hurt that his girlfriend senior year, the first girl with whom he made it to third base, revealed his big secret. His dick was enormous. It was probably eight inches long and still growing. It was extremely wide in the middle. He was too thick for some of the seniors he tried to fuck. Those girls just walked away, shaking their heads or crying from the pain. Having a big dick made it easy to get the girls into his bed, but it wasn't easy to keep them there. Many of them gave up.

Buck was average smart. He didn't get great grades and wasn't up for any scholarships. His dad was a tailor, and his mom was a housewife; they couldn't afford to send him to college. He thought about the local agricultural two-year college, which was almost affordable, but he didn't want to keep learning. He wanted to see the world.

Buck's best friend, Chet Bayer, was an Air Force brat. His father, Willy Bayer, was stationed at Warren AFB in Cheyenne. Buck admired the discipline of the military and felt a kinship with Chet's father that he hadn't found with his own dad. As graduation approached, Buck asked to speak with Willy about a career in the military. Chet arranged it, then went off to his room to do homework, leaving them in the living room to talk.

"You wanna join the forces, son?"

Buck nodded. "Yes, Mr. Bayer, I do."

"Call me Willy, please." The older man sat beside Buck on the couch and touched his knee. "Which branch do you think is right? Marines?"

Buck shrugged. "I thought maybe you'd know."

"How are your math skills?"

Buck said, "Average. I get Bs and Cs."

Willy shook his head. "Okay, so the Air Force is out. Do you like the ocean?"

Buck smiled. "Don't know. I've never been."

Willy sighed. "Let's cross off the Navy, Coast Guard, and I guess the Marines, too."

Buck said, "I guess that leaves the Army."

Willy patted Buck's leg. "Yes, son, I think you're gonna be regular Army. Ain't no shame in it. You know the slogan.'Choice, not Chance.' You'll have a big leg up in your career after active duty. If you're lucky, you'll see Europe or the Far East."

To Buck, it sounded like heaven. Willy was leaving out a lot of the unpleasant details. His hand remained on Buck's leg, which seemed odd.

Then Willy did something unexpected. His hand moved to the point on Buck's leg where his dick pressed through the fabric. He rubbed softly. Buck was eighteen. He was so horny; even this older man's touch was enough to make him rock hard in seconds.

Willy's eyes opened wide. "Whoa, son. You're packing a lot there."

Buck was confused. This guy was Chet's dad. His wife was right in the kitchen cooking dinner. How could he be acting queer like this?

Willy chuckled. "Don't try to tell me you don't like it. I was gonna suck it, but it's too big."

Buck scooted away from the handsome older man, but only half-heartedly. He had to admit that Willy's hand felt damn good on his dick.

"You know, Buck, when you're on base, there aren't any women. I mean, maybe one or two, but most of them are bull daggers, and they won't want anything to do with you."

Buck didn't know what a bull dagger was, but he figured it had to do with not liking men. "Uh, sir, what's happening here?"

Willy squeezed Buck's fat cock through his jeans. "I'm gonna show you how we do it when there's no women around. You gotta stay sane, son. Come on."

Willy ushered Buck into the guest bedroom and shut the door. He removed his shirt and pants. His briefs were like a sideways tent, stretching and straining against Willy's modest cock.

"Show me what you got, Buck."

Buck was flustered. He didn't know how he'd ended up in this queer game with Chet's dad and hated how excited it made him. He looked at Willy's face. It was strong, intelligent, and handsome. Willy's body was muscular like Buck's, but he had soft brown hair on his pecs and belly.

Buck took off his t-shirt, revealing his own thick frame. Translucent blond hairs surrounded his nipples, and a nearly invisible treasure trail ran from his belly button to his massive crotch. When Buck took off his jeans, Willy whistled.

"Damn, son, I see why you don't wear underwear. Ain't nothing gonna hold that sonofabitch in place!"

Buck's dick stood straight out, defying gravity. Willy put a hand in his briefs and stroked his much smaller dick.

"I thought I was gonna let you fuck me, but I don't think it'll work. I'm out of practice. How about I break you in?"

Buck was way out of his depth. Fuck? Asses are for shitting, not for dicks. That's what his biology teacher taught them. It was against nature, or so he said. He was pretty sure the Bible was against it, too.

Willy saw the fear wash over Buck. "Don't worry, son. It's gonna feel so good; you'll wonder why you didn't try it sooner." He stood next to Buck, caressing the fantastic thick dick. Buck was surprised to see some precum dribbling out. The prospect of a different type of sexual experience was titillating.

Willy pulled down his briefs, exposing a small but very tidy penis. He was half-hard, jerking himself to get harder. His belly fur brushed against Buck's smooth skin, causing the boy to tingle.

"What the fuck," Buck thought, "nobody needs to know." He was so horny that he started to wonder if maybe he was queer. The girls, with their soft, squishy skin, didn't make him tingle like that. Their big boobs got him hard, but they didn't excite him the way Willy's furry body did. Then, things went through the roof.

Willy knelt and planted his mouth on Buck's asshole. He had to spread the downy white cheeks far apart to reach it; they were so big and round. Willy silently tongued the hairless hole. Buck's knees buckled from the intense pleasure. He'd never felt anything like it.

"I gotta lie down, Willy; it's too good."

Buck got on the bed, on his back, and put his legs over Willy's shoulders. Willy went to town, slipping and sliding in and out of the tight pucker. At last, he pulled back, standing, lifting Buck's thick legs into the air.

"You ready? It won't hurt but a minute."

Buck didn't know what that meant. "No, sir. What'd you mean?"

"I'm gonna stick my dick in there." Willy squeezed a bit of Brylcreem onto his dick and slicked it up. "Trust me, you're gonna like this, son."

Buck was terrified. Willy's cock was dwarfed by his, but it still looked bigger than a piece of shit. There was no way it would feel good. Willy stepped forward, holding Buck's backside open, and pressed his head until it just touched the slippery hole. Buck's butt was so big it made it tricky for the older man to maneuver.

"Is it in?" Buck was surprised when he didn't feel anything.

"No, son. It's gonna burn for a bit, but it'll get better. A lot better."

Willy stepped forward again, pressing his head against the tight hole until it popped past the inner ring.

"Ow, fuck!" Buck hissed it. He didn't want Mrs. Bayer or Chet to hear his cries. He would die of embarrassment if one of them caught him like this. The burning sensation got worse as Willy pushed the rest of the way. His hips pressed against Buck's round globe of an ass. He stopped there, waiting for Buck to adjust.

"Does it still hurt?"

Buck nodded. Willy waited patiently, moving slowly in tiny strokes to keep his cock hard. "How about now?"

Buck sighed. "It's okay, I guess."

Willy picked up speed and increased the length of his strokes. He kept popping out because he lost so much of his shaft between Buck's big ass cheeks. He didn't miss a beat, just poking the little thing right back inside the slippery hole.

Buck was stunned. The way Willy's dick pushed up against a particular spot in his butt sent him over the moon. His eyes rolled around, and his big, fat cock leaked pre-cum. He didn't dare jerk off for fear he would come, and it would all be over in a flash. The giant cock throbbed, pointing skyward, wobbling as Willy's rougher and rougher strokes shook Buck's body. He only held it to steady it, and even that slight touch pushed him toward the precipice. He had to let go.

Willy smiled. "You're close, ain'tcha?"

Buck nodded. "Feels good, sir."

Willy laughed. "You don't have to call me 'sir,' kid. I'm Willy, remember?

But Buck was too deep in ecstasy to remember much of anything. Willy's hot dad's sweat dripped from his forehead onto Buck's belly. It smelled musky and masculine. The scent was what pushed Buck past the point of no return. With almost no warning, Buck felt his balls churning and pulling up tight.

"Oh, shit, Willy, I'm coming!"

Willy said, "Me too."

Buck's cock unleashed a fountain of cum that hit Willy right in the face before cascading down onto Buck's legs, belly, and crotch. A second spurt flew over his head, splattering all over the headboard.

"Holy shit, kid. You're a fuckin' firehose! Oh, god, that's hot."

Willy pressed hard, holding himself inside Buck as the boy continued to paint the room with his cum. "Oh, yeah!"

Buck felt a warm river flowing up his bum. Willy's little cock and balls churned out baby gravy in six or seven spurts. Buck was still spraying his cum when Willy's bursts subsided.

Buck stared wide-eyed at Chet's dad. His chest was beaded with sweat, which trickled down the chest hairs and pattered on Buck's body. He'd never felt this good.

All the sex with girls was child's play compared to this sweaty mix of manly fluids. When Willy pulled back, his little dick flopped out. With a little fart, Buck expelled the Bayer seed onto the bedspread.

Willy wiped himself down with a brown hand towel before pulling up his briefs and putting on his trousers. He threw the towel to Buck.

"Clean up. Don't forget your ass. No wet spots back there, right?"

Buck smiled and wiped himself down. He got up to wipe the headboard, but Willy stopped him. "Let the cleaning lady do it."

The two men returned to the living room, flushed. Mrs. Bayer was busy making dinner and didn't leave the kitchen.

"What's for dinner, honey?"

She said, "Irish Stew."

Willy licked his lips. "Why don't you stay for supper? Maybe I can give you dessert later."

JUDD THE BULLY

Buck wrestled with his thoughts after that encounter. He didn't look at girls the same way anymore. Instead, the cherubic young man started noticing the jocks and cowboys. He was surprised to see a few of them looking back.

One particularly nasty cowboy named Judd Grimes caught Buck looking at him. "Whatcha looking at, faggot?"

Buck gasped. He was used to looking at whatever guy he wanted; he hadn't imagined anyone would notice.

"Uh, nothing, Judd." He thought fast. "I think you might have some ketchup on your jeans."

He ran off, leaving Judd twirling and twisting, trying to find the stain. "You better run, faggot!" Judd snarled as he watched Buck's ass bouncing away.

After school, Judd cornered Buck. "You're queer."

Buck shook his head. Judd was much taller than Buck but skinnier. Buck figured it would be a fair fight if it came to that. "I didn't find no ketchup on me. You was looking at this."

He grabbed his dick through his pants. Buck couldn't help but glance down, and what he saw was very long.

Judd pushed closer to Buck. He could smell the tobacco on his breath when he said, "I see you. You want this, don't you."

They were in a corner of the school with very little foot traffic. But just then, Dolores Quant, Buck's ex, rounded the corner.

She stomped her foot. "Lay off him, Judd Grimes."

Judd spat dark brown tobacco juice between Buck's feet. "I'm watching you, faggot."

There were only a few weeks until graduation, and Buck dreaded every day. Judd tripped him, spit on him, and made his life hell. Then it changed.

On the first Friday in May, Buck went to take a piss between classes. He heard the door slam open, and Judd walked in.

"Well, well. If it isn't my little queer buddy!" The bully locked the door behind him.

Buck felt panic rise. He didn't like fighting. Judd came at him with a fist. Buck was still in the middle of pissing. He ducked to avoid Judd, and his big cock swung around, splashing Judd's jeans. He held tight, trying not to piss anymore.

Then Judd acted crazy. He got down near Buck's dick and said, "Fuck, you're big! Do it. Finish it up on my face."

Buck hesitated. "Uh, what do you mean?"

Judd sucked his teeth. "Fuckin' piss in my mouth, man! Hurry up!"

Buck let loose and finished up in Judd's mouth. He watched, fascinated, as his personal terrorist became a strange, submissive urinal. Judd drank it down.

"If you fuckin' tell anyone, I'll beat you to death." The bell rang.

Buck said, "Uh, Judd, I gotta get to class."

Judd shook his head. "No way. You and me ain't finished yet."

He pushed Buck into a stall, his face still dripping

wet with piss. He rubbed Buck's hole through his jeans. "You got a sweet ass, little man. I'm gonna fuck the shit out of you."

Judd pulled down his jeans, revealing a very long, skinny cock. It was longer than Buck's but only as big around as Willy's. The cowboy spat tobacco on his cock, slicking it up. He spit near Buck's hole and wiped it with his thumb.

"Get ready, punk. This is gonna hurt."

It didn't. The thin cock slipped smoothly into Buck's ass. Judd gave a nasty chuckle. "Whadda ya know? You are a little faggot. You like it!"

Buck nodded. He did, and he didn't care. "Shut up and fuck me, Judd."

Buck felt a new sensation. Judd was so long that he pushed through a hole Buck didn't even know existed. It felt good, but the awkward angle in the toilet made it hard for Buck to enjoy much.

It was fast. Eighteen-year-olds' hormones don't wait for anyone. In less than a minute, Judd shot a load way up in Buck's ass. He didn't wait for Buck to come. He zipped up, unlocked the bathroom, and headed out into the hall. Buck sat on the toilet until the deeply planted seeds trickled out. He wiped up and limped to class late.

After that bathroom encounter, Judd tried to pursue Buck, who avoided him as much as possible. He didn't want to have sex with him again. He pissed in his mouth a few times, but it wasn't really his thing. Judd wasn't a thoughtful lover like Willy Bayer. He was a selfish prick. The few times they fucked in the stalls, Buck just let Judd have him. He didn't try to get off, and Judd didn't care. All he wanted was a fat ass to dump his load. Buck didn't much care. He simply let the wiry cowboy unload in his ass. He was just glad Judd wasn't trying to beat him up anymore. The last bell of Buck's school career rang, and it couldn't have come soon enough.

❧ 3 ❧

NED ON THE BUS

Buck sat on the back of the bus to Fort Knox. It was a long ride — nearly twenty-four hours. Graduation had been less than a week ago, and already he was on his way to a new adventure. He looked around the bus, wondering if anyone else was off to boot camp like him. Nebraska was hypnotic. He saw nothing but corn out both sides of the bus. It put him to sleep. When he woke up, they were in Omaha. The city was much bigger than Cheyenne, with a few sky-scrapers and many green spaces. The men who boarded here were Midwestern giants. "They must feed them well in Omaha," Buck thought.

A handsome businessman in a tight suit sat across from Buck and tipped his fedora. He stood and re-moved his jacket, then pulled the legs of his suit, trying to get it to stop creeping up. Buck got a glimpse of his crotch and gasped aloud. It was a huge bulge the size of a softball.

The businessman winked at Buck and adjusted him-self. "Damn suit's like a straitjacket for my crotch!"

Buck was surprised that a stranger would talk about his private parts like that. When the man sat, he put one hand on the mound between his legs and stroked it with his thumb. The bus took off. Buck felt his khakis grow tight as his cock plumped up. He had to stand and adjust, too.

The businessman whistled. "Holy shit, kid, that's a big one!"

Buck blushed and sat down. He wondered what the man's cock looked like. It was just a big blob between his legs.

"Mind if I sit next to you?"

Buck looked around. There was nobody else back there with them. "Yeah, sure."

When the guy stood, his bulge seemed to move of its own accord. The man's muscles were huge; the seams of his shirt looked ready to burst. The man loosened his tie as he slid across the aisle to sit beside Buck. "Name's Ned." He shook Buck's hand. He didn't waste any time. He opened Buck's jeans and pulled out his throbbing cock.

"Holy cow. That's too big!"

Buck sighed. He'd heard it too many times. Mostly from girls, but now the guys were saying it, too. "Yeah, sorry."

Ned said, "I'm gonna give it the old college try." He leaned over Buck's lap and put the big head in his mouth. He swirled his tongue over it. Buck had been with enough girls to know that a blow job was out of the question. But the man surprised him. He shoved down and took another few inches of Buck into his mouth. It felt better than any damn girl.

"Oh, god. That feels good."

"Mmmhmm." Ned agreed. He bobbed up and down, using his tongue to stimulate Buck's head.

Buck shifted in his seat. "I'm gonna come."

Ned kept sucking and licking. Buck hadn't jacked off in a few days, so his balls were full. He jerked his hips several times, then unloaded in Ned's mouth. The businessman gulped it down hungrily, not letting a single drop spill.

Ned said, "Can I fuck you?"

Buck wanted it but wasn't sure something as big as a softball would feel good. "Can I see?"

Ned shrugged and unzipped his tight suit pants. He reached deep and pulled out a packed pair of briefs. He tugged down, revealing a short, incredibly thick cock. It was nearly as big around as the broad middle of Buck's dick.

Buck failed to suppress a groan.

The business guy shrugged, ready to put it away.

Buck grabbed his hand. "Wait. I want to try."

"You'll suck it?"

Buck shook his head. "I want you to fuck me."

The businessman's face lit up. "You mean it? We can go in there." He pointed to the tiny toilet behind them. He reached into his jacket pocket and produced a small tube of Vaseline. "I come prepared."

Ned stood first and entered the toilet. Buck waited two minutes before squeezing in. Ned was a massive man; there was barely enough room for Buck. They maneuvered until Buck was over the toilet, holding the bar to steady himself. The bus rocked from side to side as it careened down the lonely highway toward Kansas City. Buck couldn't see anything but felt Ned's warm, greasy hand on his hole. He put a finger in, then two, then three. Buck groaned. He'd only had skinny dicks up there. Ned's fat fingers were taking him to new heights.

When he put in a fourth, Buck protested. "Ow!"

Ned didn't stop. He kept pushing his four fingers back and forth in a rhythm. Buck felt his ass loosen. Then Ned added his thumb. Buck saw stars.

"You ain't that big, are you?" Buck was hoping not.

Ned said, "Let's just say it's better if you let me keep going. It'll be easier. Trust me, I'm an expert."

Buck felt a colossal burst of pain as Ned pushed his whole fat fist into him. But the pain was overshadowed by a peculiar sense of connection. There was an intimacy in being held from the inside. Ned punched a few times. Each time it made a popping sound that made Buck's spent cock grow rock hard again.

"You're ready." Ned pulled out his greasy fist, wiping the outside on the cloth towel dispenser and using his palm to slick up his cock. Buck couldn't see what was coming, and it excited him. He wanted to be surprised.

The head that pressed at his hole was the size of a cue ball. Buck thought he would rip in two when Ned pushed it in. The shaft was the same thickness, so Ned slid back in a smooth, graceful glide. His cock stopped at the back of the rectum as Ned's hips pressed against Buck's fat ass. He was maybe six inches at most but felt like nine inches around. The pressure caused Buck's cock to churn out a steady stream of pre-cum that stretched downward until it pooled on the toilet seat.

Buck had only just learned how to get fucked. Ned's giant prick was way more challenging than Willy or Judd. Chet's father, with his smaller-than-average cock prepared him for Judd's long, thin, garter snake cock. But nothing had prepared him for Ned's beer-can-shaped cock. Every second that passed felt like an hour. Buck cried softly to himself, praying for relief. His prayers were answered.

Ned pulled out halfway, then plunged in again. This sliding motion afforded Buck some relief from the gut-ripping pain. The more Ned did it, the easier it became to tolerate it. Then, it went from tolerance to enjoyment. When Ned started fucking at a breakneck pace, it sent Buck into spasms of pleasure. He could feel the muscles in his butt cheeks contracting involuntarily. His hard dick cried out for release, but he couldn't reach it in the cramped space. It was like fucking in the back-seat of a sports car. Not being able to touch himself, he experienced a new kind of pleasure. The intense pressure and friction in his asshole made him quiver. His cock throbbed and drooled. He felt his balls moving on their own in a dance whose beats came from the steady smack, smack of Ned's cock against the rear wall of Buck's hole.

"That feels so good." Buck was barely able to squeak out those words. His whole body was wracked with pleasure.

"Same here."

With those words, Buck realized what he loved about getting fucked. He gave men just as much pleasure as they gave him. It was an even exchange. Ned's fat cock throbbed inside him, pounding at his bladder. To his surprise, Buck began to pee. Ned was fucking the piss right out of him. His long cock was hovering right over the toilet bowl; it was perfect. Buck cried out. The force against his bladder broke through the pleasure in a little burst of pain. And then it was gone.

"You okay?" Ned sounded half-interested in Buck's well-being.

"Yeah," Buck said, "I'm pissing myself, but I'm good."

Ned laughed. "Happens all the time. Don't worry, it'll stop."

Buck expelled the last droplets of urine, and everything returned to pleasure and lust. Buck pushed back to meet Ned's thrusts. Buck was hooked. He could've fucked all the way to St. Louis. But someone was eventually going to come knocking, and Ned knew it.

"You ready for my load, boy?"

"Yes, sir." Buck wished he could jack himself off. His cock throbbed and shook with each blow from behind. Ned was punching Buck in the guts via his ass.

"Oh, son, it's coming."

Buck liked being called 'son.' It turned him on. He tried to get one hand between his legs to jack off, but he couldn't. The cramped toilet was too small for him to move much at all.

"Oh, shit! Here it comes." Ned stopped pounding

and held himself all the way inside Buck. The flood of cum in Buck's guts had nowhere to go. With a loud raspberry, the cum squirted out around the sides of Ned's fat cock.

Buck surprised himself. Ned's sudden stop pushed Buck over a precipice he hadn't seen coming. His cock shot sperm all over the toilet and the wall in front of him. As his overstuffed ass spewed cum on Ned's tight suit pants, Buck painted the tiny room with his cock.

Ned held Buck around the chest and squeezed. "Thank you." He kissed the back of Buck's neck and yanked his pants up. He wiped them with his hand, trying to clean the cum off. It didn't work.

"Oh well. It'll dry." He opened the bathroom door and stepped out into the aisle. "Stay in there a minute or two."

Buck moved around in the cramped space, dripping cum from the front and back. The toilet paper roll was empty, so he had to wait until the cum dried, which it did quickly.

As he pulled his pants up, there was a knock at the door.

"Just a minute!" He zipped up and opened the door. It was a hefty midwestern church lady in a bonnet and a sun dress. She looked past Buck and saw the mess.

"Oh, land's sake. Was it like that when you went in?"

Buck smiled. "Yes, ma'am. Ain't no towels, neither, so I can't rightly clean it up."

"Disgusting. I have some tissues in my purse." She waddled into the tiny toilet, barely big enough to hold her wide bottom, then locked the door. Buck felt bad. He returned to his seat. Ned was back on the other side of the aisle, eyes closed, snoring.

4
BOOT CAMP

Buck got off the bus at 9 a.m. in Fort Knox and found a dark green army bus waiting for him and a couple of dozen other young men who had come from all directions. A grey-haired drill sergeant barked orders.

"You will call me Sergeant Dixon. Let's go, recruits. Go! Go! Go! It's go-time! Double-time, men! If you're not on that bus in 30 seconds, you'll be sorry!" The recruits crowded the entrance to the bus, everyone pushing to be first. Sergeant Dixon grabbed the first to climb aboard ahead of the mob and pushed him out. "You gotta learn teamwork! These are your fellow soldiers. Cooperate!" It took several tries, but they finally organized into a single file, and when the Sergeant blew his whistle, they quickly filed onto the bus just before the 30-second whistle blew.

Sergeant Dixon didn't smile. "You're a bunch of pathetic fools. It took you four tries to figure that out. This is my worst squad yet!"

From that moment forward, Buck realized his days would be nothing but orders, drills, hurried meals, and insufficient sleep. He hadn't imagined how much more it would be.

When they got to Fort Knox, Sergeant Dixon hustled them off the bus and into a room where all their duffle bags were in a single pile. Through teamwork, every soldier found their bag. In the next room, Buck was assigned a bunk and issued a wool blanket, two flat bed sheets, a razor-thin pillow, and dark green army fatigues.

The first stop was the showers. Buck saw the same look of bewilderment on the face of every recruit. They were painfully aware they had given up their freedom in exchange for a few dollars a month, constant berating, and an uncomfortable bed.

Sergeant Dixon shouted, "Strip! Men, you got six minutes!"

As Buck stripped, he looked around at the other guys. Short, fat, tall, skinny, ugly, handsome — they were a rainbow of the masculine form. Buck stripped off his jeans and folded them on the bench. He heard catcalls and turned to see the whole room staring at his big, soft cock.

"Holy H-E-double hockey sticks!" A short, skinny, pimply-faced Southerner stared brazenly at Buck's dick. "You part horse?"

There were snickers and jeers. Buck reddened, turning away, trying to hide what was too big to be hidden.

An olive-skinned New Yorker with shiny black hair, rippling muscles, and piercing green eyes stepped between Buck and the laughing crowd. "Hey, knock it off! The guy can't help it." The young man's immense muscles intimidated the onlookers. They quieted down and went back to their showers.

Sergeant Dixon nodded at the New Yorker. "Good job protecting your buddy."

Buck whispered. "Thank you." He couldn't help but glance down. To his surprise, the guy was so small down there that it almost looked like a pussy.

"Yeah, no problem. Yo, I got the opposite problem, right?"

Buck looked down again. "Yeah."

The green-eyed muscleman extended his hand. "Vinnie. Vinnie DiFranco."

"Buck Hartigan." When Buck took Vinnie's hand, he felt how small it was, yet at the same time so powerful. They hit the showers. There were only enough heads for two to share. Buck let the New Yorker go first.

Vinnie's eyes twinkled. "God don't hand out nothing equal, am I right?"

Buck smiled. "Too much of a good thing is as bad as not enough."

Vinnie lathered up. His tiny penis disappeared in the soap bubbles. Nothing Buck could do would ever hide his huge cock. He envied Vinnie. It was mutual, no doubt. The New Yorker didn't try to hide his fascination with Buck's appendage.

"You fuck girls with that?"

Buck shrugged. "Not anymore. You?"

Vinnie laughed. "Nope." The silence that followed spoke volumes. They both knew.

Buck said, "You sure have a great body. I mean, you must work out every day."

Vinnie smiled proudly. "I do. Gotta look good." He dropped the soap, probably on purpose, and bent down to pick it up, revealing a creamy, white, muscular butt. It was as big as Buck's but hard with muscle. Between the cheeks, Buck could see Vinnie's hole, which looked a little saggy, like it had been used a lot. Buck felt a hard-on growing between his legs.

Vinnie stood up and looked down. "Yeah, I thought so." He tossed the soap at Buck, who caught it and then dropped it.

Buck bent over to retrieve it, and Vinnie whistled. "I like that view." The room's sound level increased with young men showering, laughing, yelling. None of them paid any attention to Buck and Vinnie's conversation. Buck knew that would end if he got hard. Vinnie stood between Buck and the other guys, blocking any view of his dick.

"I see you got a problem coming on. Here." He tossed Buck a towel. "Get dressed. We can talk later."

Sergeant Dixon cut off the showers at six minutes. Buck still had soap in his eyes. They had 60 seconds to dry off, and it was on to the barber if you could call it that. Buck watched his beautiful, curly blond locks fall to the floor, mixed with the hair of a dozen other recruits. They were ordered to their bunks to put their things away.

Buck found his bunk. The pimply Southerner had already claimed the top bunk. "I don't want none of y'all's farts in my face."

Buck laughed. "I'll climb up there and lay one on you."

The boy smiled. "Better not! I'm Aloysius Sherman from Natchez, Mississippi."

"Buck Hartigan from Cheyenne."

"You got the biggest fuckin' dick I never seen in my life." Aloysius's Southern drawl and bad grammar were slow and lyrical.

Buck said, "I didn't have much to do with it."

Aloysius nodded. "That's the Lord's work right there. Yessir. He blessed you good. He did alright by me." Aloysius grabbed his crotch. It looked substantial for such a short kid. "You got a girl back home, Buck?"

"Nah. I did, but, uh, yeah. I did."

Aloysius leaned his head on his hand. "I don't neither. Girls don't really like me."

Buck didn't think. "But do you like them?" It sounded rude when it came out of his mouth.

Aloysius said, "Fuck yeah. I love pussy. Why?" Buck

heard a slight note of insincerity in his bunkmate's voice.

Buck said, "Sorry, man. I didn't mean to ask that."

"You queer?"

"What?" Buck blushed.

"I asked if you was queer." Aloysius didn't sound threatening or judgmental. He appeared curious and maybe interested.

Buck said, "Maybe."

Aloysius clapped his hands together hard. "I knew it! Don't worry, your secret's safe with me. To tell you the truth, I'm a little bit queer myself. Don't tell no one."

Buck was dumbstruck. He'd already met two queers in less than an hour. Willy Bayer had been right. Military men were all a little queer.

Sergeant Dixon appeared, red in the face. "Stop jabbering! We got work to do!" He hustled them out in the blazing heat to a hot spot of pavement, where three dozen men did pushups until they collapsed. Buck thought he was going to die.

5

LITTLE VINNIE GOES DEEP

Aloysius sat with Buck at dinner. Vinnie joined them. They all looked awful with their newly bald heads.

"Gentlemen." The thick New York accent was charming. It sounded like, "Gen-oh-men".

The food was awful—creamed chipped beef on toast. Shit-on-a-shingle, they called it.

Sergeant Dixon made an announcement. "No empty plates, men. Eat up! Every empty plate I find'll be twenty pushups for the whole regiment. Buck hadn't eaten in hours, so he forced himself to finish dinner.

Buck liked Vinnie, and he didn't hate Aloysius. They talked about home, better food, city life, and country life. Then Dixon shouted at them. He counted the unfinished plates and announced there would be 220 pushups before bed. And he made sure to call out everybody's name, including little Aloysius, who couldn't finish because his stomach was too small. Buck was sick of the Army on his first day.

After cleaning the quarters, At 8 pm, Dixon gave the men one hour of PT (Personal Time) before the 9 pm lights out. Vinnie's eyes sparkled. "I gotta go to the can." He motioned for Buck to follow him. He passed the toilet in their barracks and walked Buck to barracks that would be empty for two weeks until a new batch arrived. He and Buck shared a stall and whispered.

Vinnie said, "Show me that ass."

Buck smiled. "You know you can't fuck me."

"I got dis thing I do. Now drop 'em."

Buck dropped his fatigues. Vinnie knelt and pulled down the briefs, exposing Buck's huge round ass. Buck gulped when he felt Vinnie's tongue touch his anus. He spread his legs and held his cheeks to let Vinnie in.

"Oh, fuck, champ. Ya got a helluva ass!" He quieted down as his tongue got busy in Buck's hole.

Buck hadn't felt a tongue like Vinnie's before. It was so long that it felt like a little penis. Buck reached behind him, between his legs, to stroke Vinnie's little penis, but the muscleman slapped him away.

"Mmm-mm!" Vinnie scolded Buck without words. He licked and prodded Buck for several minutes, then pulled back. "You taste good. Okay, get ready."

From the corner of his eye, Buck saw Vinnie holding a tube of cream. He felt it on his ass. Then, without warning, Vinnie shoved his whole fist into Buck's ass. His tiny hands were still huge inside his ass. Buck stifled a yelp of pain.

"The worst is over. Just hold on. It'll be better in a sec."

Vinnie was right. The muscular hunk had a slim wrist, and it stopped hurting. Instead, Buck felt fantastic. Vinnie's fist pressed against his prostate. Buck sighed.

When Vinnie pushed forward, his massive forearm stretched Buck wide. But it didn't hurt much. Vinnie punched Buck's guts in a steady rhythm. Buck groaned, dripping precum from his massive cock. Vinnie reached forward with his free hand and milked Buck like a cow.

"Careful, I'm about to..." Buck had no time to finish. He shot a massive load on the rim of the toilet. Looking behind him, he saw Vinnie shoot his tiny load on the floor without touching himself. It turned him on.

"Let me fuck you, Vinnie."

"Hell no! I don't let nothing in here. Not even a tongue. Last thing went in there got chopped off!"

Buck was taken aback, but he chuckled. "A carrot?"

They both laughed as Vinnie washed off the grease from his arm with the Boraxo soap powder.

They made it back to the barracks just before lights out. Buck limped to his lower bunk. Aloysius stuck his head down to talk to Buck.

"Where'd you two go?"

Buck wasn't sure what to tell the kid.

❅ 6 ❅

SARGE'S NEW GRUNT

L ike a waking nightmare, Sergeant Dixon's angry shouts and taunts startled Buck from his sleep.

"Go! Go! Go! Triple-time! I want these beds made and ready for inspection in two minutes! I'd better be able to bounce a quarter off the bed, or you're coming with me!"

Buck struggled with the two flat sheets. He knew hospital corners, but they always took him a while. Still, he got his bed neat and tight before two minutes was up.

As the sergeant made his rounds, Buck looked around the room. The whole squad was in varying states of undress. His bunkmate Aloysius stood beside him with nothing on but the skin God made him. Buck marveled at the little man's cock, which swung like a pendulum between his knees. Every time he stole a glance, he felt his own massive beast swell. Buck was getting hard during inspection! He tried to think of something else but couldn't quiet his mind enough to get his bunkmate's prodigious penis out of there. Aloysius was hit with the ugly stick, but God apologized in the form of a giant cock.

Sergeant Dixon came around with a quarter. Buck

swallowed hard. His boxers were straining against his hard-on. He waited for his CO to humiliate him. He didn't.

The drill sergeant leaned in and whispered in Buck's ear. "Watch this."

He threw the quarter at the bed in such a way that it wouldn't have bounced in a million years.

"Hartigan! That's one demerit. Put on some clothes, go to my office, and wait there!"

As Buck stumbled towards the CO's suite, he heard the sergeant berating Aloysius, too. "Sherman! This bed is a sorry excuse. Meet me in the office!"

The two men, in fatigues and white t-shirts, sat in Sergeant Dixon's office, waiting for whatever torture he had in store for them. Aloysius couldn't hide his terror. He was a nervous talker, too.

"Oh shit, Buck, what's he gonna do? Are we getting kicked out?"

Buck thought that would be too merciful. "No, he probably's gonna give us some shitty, meaningless crap to do."

Aloysius was a bundle of nerves. His legs bounced up and down. Buck marveled at how the soft, thick cock bounced in his bunkmate's fatigues. He felt that unwelcome surge of arousal creeping back.

Aloysius said, "I'm not so sure, man. He's so mean."

The sergeant entered the room. "Who's mean, son?"

Aloysius looked ready to collapse. "Uh, my dad."

"Look, Al, you can stop worrying. I got you in here to keep you safe. I know you weren't talking about your dad. And Buck, the 'crap' I give you won't be meaningless, I assure you." He shut the door.

Both men blushed as they realized they'd been busted even worse, talking shit about the Sarge.

The older man put his hands on his hips, then adjusted his crotch. Buck saw a long lump growing down one pant leg. The sergeant was a perv, too!

"Buck, I'll bet my bottom dollar you've been through this drill before. You got that look." He turned to the shorter man. "Al, I'm not so sure with you. You take it up the ass before?"

Aloysius turned beet red. "What? No! I fucked some ass, but I ain't no queer."

The sergeant nodded. He unbuttoned his pants and gestured for the two men to do the same. He smiled at Buck. "You didn't protest. I know you got a pussy back there, sure as shit. Am I right?"

Buck was confused by the language, but he nodded. "Yeah, I guess so."

The sergeant's eyes lit up. "Good. This is just how I like it. I'm gonna watch you get fucked by that," he pointed to the horse cock emerging from Aloysius's fatigues, "and then I'm gonna take you to paradise."

Buck knew this wasn't in any Army manual in any country in the world. He felt aroused and helpless in equal measure. He couldn't hide the boner that thickened between his legs. He felt betrayed by the way Aloysius grinned in eager anticipation as he rubbed his cock to warm it up. The Sarge handed the boy a tub of margarine. Aloysius knew just what to do. He slicked up his cock, and wiped the rest on Buck's backside.

"Assume the position, men!" Buck had enough experience to know that his position was arms outstretched, braced against the desk, his ass low enough for Aloysius to enter. Buck was still tingling from Frank's fist the night before. It made everything a little easier. Al was hung huge, but he was not longer than Frank's forearm and definitely not as thick. He was astonished at how easily the boy entered him. Even the Sergeant gave a surprised gasp.

"Shit, son, you're a pro. Good work, Grunt! You'll make Private yet."

Buck felt a strange blend of shame and pride. He felt like he'd done something right for the first time, yet he was sure it was something dirty and wrong. Why did it have to feel so good? Aloysius humped him, pounding into his rectum. With a twist, Buck let him slide past into the colon.

"Oh shit, Buck, did I hurt you?"

Buck felt discomfort but not pain. He shook his head.

The sergeant's cock was trapped in his pant leg. He rubbed it with an amazed expression on his face. He patted Buck on the back with his free hand. "You're blessed, boy."

Aloysius took advantage of his new-found freedom, fucking Buck in long, luxurious strokes. "Oh damn, Buck. Ain't no pussy in the world can do this!"

Buck chuckled to himself. He doubted Aloysius had ever been in a woman before. Between his ugly face and his obscene endowment, he would have scared off any of them.

Buck finally got a glimpse of the sergeant's bulge straining against the fabric of his khakis. It hadn't been much the last time he looked. Now, it was more than halfway to his knee and as thick as Vinnie's muscular forearm. It was brutal.

The sergeant struggled to free the monster from its khaki cage. When it finally broke free, it flew upward, hitting Buck square on the chin like a knockout punch. Buck's jaw dropped. Sarge's cock was thicker than Buck's widest spot and at least an inch longer, too. It was a perfect cylinder, topped with a wide head. Buck worried how it would feel inside him. It helped that his bunkmate was pounding him while he stared at it. It gave him confidence.

"You think you can suck it, get it harder?"

Buck didn't know, but he wanted to find out. He opened his mouth wide and engulfed the head. It pressed out against his cheeks. He struggled to get air to move past it and had to breathe through his nose.

But the sergeant leaned back and said, "Oh, yeah, like that! Shit!"

To Buck's surprise, the head hardened and swelled even further. He felt his lips stretch until the corners cracked. To ease the discomfort, Buck pushed the head further back until it touched his tonsils. He gagged but got it under control.

"Hey, hey, Grunt. You don't have to do that. It's impossible. Trust me. I know."

Buck hated the Army, but he loved the attention he was getting. He wanted to keep his drill sergeant happy. He took a deep breath and went for it. With great effort, he felt the massive head move past his tonsils and down his throat. He immediately regretted it. His throat screamed with agony.

"Oh fuck, how did you do that? No one ever - oh!"

Buck was turned on by how much he'd surprised Sarge, and he kept forcing more and more meat down his throat until his nose felt the tickle of pubic hair on his nostrils. Stuffed full at both ends, Buck had found his happy spot. This was heaven. For now. He cupped Dixon's heavy balls in his hand and squeezed.

"Oh, son, that feels too good. I got more in store for you." He pushed Buck off of his dick, which dripped with gooey saliva.

Aloysius was young, dumb, and full of cum. He held himself inside Buck and blasted his guts with an endless torrent of Southern baby juice. Buck was glad he couldn't see his bunkmate's ugly face contort with orgasm. He loved the deep, warm flow in his belly, and that was all. Aloysius was a lousy lay, despite having a huge cock. His technique needed work. He pulled out of Buck, dumping a load of his sperm onto the linoleum floor.

Sarge pushed Aloysius away and put the tip of his huge, wet dick between Buck's gorgeous, round butt cheeks. "You ready for paradise, son?"

Buck nodded. He loved it when men called him son. It satisfied his soul.

Not even Vinnie's forearm could have prepared Buck for the assault on his anus. Sarge slowly forced the tip of his enormous cock head into Buck, then held it there, demonstrating his experience and technique.

Aloysius came around for a cleaning, but the sergeant barked at him. "You're done here, grunt! Get dressed and go back to your bunk! He's mine now."

Buck wondered if he meant "from now on" or "just for now." He didn't have much time to ponder it when he felt the flared corona pass his sphincter with a powerful shot of pain. As the sergeant moved through him, he felt every part of his rectum stretched and pressed. Buck twisted, but the passageway wasn't wide or straight enough to allow Sarge to turn the corner. No matter. Sergeant Dixon pulled back until his corona caught on the inner ring, then pushed forward again in a long, slow slide. Buck's legs grew sticky with juice. Each stroke extracted another droplet of clear goo from his piss slit.

Sarge grunted in Buck's ear. "You like that, son? You want me to keep going."

"Yes, sir."

Sergeant Dixon needed no further encouragement. He picked up the pace, bludgeoning Buck's rectum and pushing in as far as it would allow, rearranging the boy's insides. The second hole yearned to relieve the pressure but wasn't positioned right to take the Sergeant's extra few inches. The colossal head bounced between the inner rectum and the second hole over and over, making Buck feel faint with desire and pleasure.

"You're doing great, Grunt! Are you ready for the rest?"

Buck knew he wasn't. "Sir, yes, sir!"

The sergeant lifted Buck by the waist, allowing gravity to force him through the second hole in a blinding flash of agony. Buck saw stars, and then the room went black. When he woke up, the first thing he noticed was a stapler on the desk pressing into his back. He saw a strange lump pressing up against his belly. It was Sarge's huge round cock head invading his lower abdomen. As the room came into focus, the sergeant dripped sweat. Buck saw relief wash over his face.

"Oh, you're back. Don't do that! Stay with me, soldier!"

Buck didn't like the implication that he'd lost consciousness on purpose. He had no control. The pleasures of penetration outweighed the agony in his nether regions. Buck lifted his dangling legs and wrapped them around the sergeant's waist.

"That's my boy."

Buck leaked another trickle of precum at the word "boy." The sergeant's dick was thicker than Ned's and longer than his own. He felt the heaviness as it moved through him, engorged, rock-hard, unrelenting. He'd never felt more alive, more useful. He was pleasing his drill sergeant, and he was pleasing him. The Army was cruel, but this was a moment of kindness at the very center.

Buck's soft cock lolled on his thigh. The sergeant straightened his arms, lifting his body. This allowed the grunt to see the enormous prick sliding into him. It aroused him. His cock lifted, filling the space the sergeant had created, pressing against his belly. As Sarge pounded into him, his furry tummy brushed against Buck's big dick. Buck closed his eyes, savoring the tingling sensations against his throbbing cock.

"Oh, Buck, is that your dick?" The sergeant looked down, then smiled at the grunt. "Good boy, Daddy's making you hard."

At those words, Buck went over a precipice. "I'm gonna cum, Daddy."

"It's sir!" the sergeant smacked him, which only pushed him closer to that edge.

The sergeant bludgeoned Buck's guts with his massive billy club cock. Buck felt his balls drawing up.

"It's coming, sir."

"Hold it," said the sergeant sternly.

Buck couldn't stop the growing flood. He whimpered with fear, pain, and overwhelming pleasure.

"Sir, I can't hold it."

The sergeant slapped him hard. "Hold your cum, boy."

The word "boy" was the last straw. Buck's cock throbbed; his balls drew up close. He fired off round after round of gooey hot cum. Each thrust from the sergeant pushed out another payload.

"Oh, Sarge, sir, I'm sorry."

The sergeant said, "I ain't stopping if you think that's gonna happen, son. I'm not done yet."

Buck quickly understood what the sergeant meant. The pleasure subsided, but the pain didn't go anywhere. Soon, it was agony. Buck wanted to beg him to stop, but he couldn't. He had to please his drill sergeant. He thrashed in pain.

"Next time, you'll hold it until I'm done."

Next time. Buck groaned. The fucking was good, but not in that moment. He was suffering. After five more minutes, the sergeant's breaths grew shallow. The sweat pouring off his forehead dried up. He threw his head back and yelled.

"Take it, boy!"

Buck felt the familiar flood of warmth in his colon. Every nerve was raw; the sergeant's cum was like a salve for his wounds. He relaxed as he felt the sergeant's cock shrink slowly in his guts. In a surprising moment of tenderness, the sergeant planted his mouth on Buck's and kissed him gently.

"Good boy. You're mine now. I own that ass."

"Yes, sir." Buck suppressed a groan. He felt like his whole lower digestive tract was blown out. He could barely push the sergeant's soft cock out; he was so sore. The smooth muscles contracted involuntarily, inching the monster out of Buck's colon and then his rectum. With a loud slap, the sergeant's beast slapped his thigh.

"Get your clothes on, grunt. You're late for breakfast."

7

IN THE INFIRMARY

Buck limped to the cafeteria, each step sending jolts of pain up his spine. He arrived as they were clearing breakfast. He managed to get some cold grits and eggs and eat them in the 30 remaining seconds before the whistle blew, signaling drills.

On the yard, the Sarge ignored Buck's grimaces of pain with each jumping jack, push-up, pull-up, and sit-up. Only when Buck felt a wet spot on his backside did the sergeant relent.

"Grunt, go to the infirmary, double-time!"

Buck nearly collapsed on the way to the medical facility. The nurse helped him onto a table, where he held his stomach and groaned. As he writhed and shook, he felt like he was dying.

The doctor came into the room with a clipboard and an attitude. "Oh, my, you're getting blood on the exam table! Stop moving around. Let me examine you."

The doctor lowered Buck's pants. "I see the sergeant's taken a liking to you. I've seen this before."

Buck couldn't believe his ears. The army medic was in on this, too?

The doctor continued, "The best thing you can do is suck it up and get used to it. This is just a little internal bleeding. It will heal up in a few days. I'll talk to the sergeant."

Buck lay there, incredulous. Willy Bayer had told him what happens in the service, but he didn't imagine it would be like this. The sergeant was abusing his power. The doctor was playing into his hands. Why? He found out.

"I got a little arrangement with Sarge. He owns you now, as you no doubt already heard. But he'll lend you out to certain officers like me. Don't worry, I'm not into butt stuff." The doctor unzipped his pants, producing a perfectly average, stiff penis. "Do you mind sucking this?"

Buck did mind, but he was backed into a corner. It was a quick and easy blow job. Buck spat out the doctor's cum. It tasted old and stale.

The doctor zipped up, satisfied. "I'm going to recommend you stay off the Sarge's dick for a week to give you time to heal." He wrote a note and sealed it in an envelope. "Give this directly to Sarge."

8

KITCHEN PATROL

Buck dropped the note off, then returned to his bunk. He saw Aloysius whispering to another grunt. He only caught the tail end of the conversation.

"Naw, man, I'm telling you. He's sweeter than pussy. Oh, shit, he's here. Act normal."

Buck glared at his bunkmate before lying down very carefully. His insides felt like the whole platoon had marched over them. He popped a pain pill and slowly drifted off to sleep.

During that week of healing, Sarge put Buck on KP. He still did morning drills and endurance training, but in the afternoon, while the other grunts did hard labor, Buck peeled potatoes, chopped carrots, and butchered sides of beef. On the fifth day of this unusual break, Sarge stopped by.

"How's KP?"

Buck smiled. "It's fine, Sarge."

The drill instructor grunted. "Don't get used to it, you're gonna be on Dick Patrol soon enough. Stop by my office after dinner."

Buck worried. The doctor said it would be a week, but Sarge appeared to be jumping the gun.

After dinner, Buck reported to the sergeant's office.

"Okay, Grunt, glad you're back. The doctor said a week, so we're back in business."

"Uh, sir, it's been five days."

"One business week, maggot! Now get on your knees and stuff this hog in your throat."

Buck said, "Sir, yes, sir!"

He knelt and put the baseball-sized head in his mouth, unhinging his jaws like a boa constrictor to accommodate the impossibly large cock.

"Son, you have a rare talent." Buck grew hard hearing the word "son." He was a daddy's boy, plain and simple. Sarge was a cruel father, but Buck craved his attention, even though he was angry with himself for letting this man dominate him so cruelly. But he had no time for dwelling on his feelings. He had a club of a cock to slick up with his throat juices.

"That's the way, son. Get it hard and wet." Sarge held the back of Buck's head, allowing him infrequent gasps of air.

After several minutes, as Buck thought he might pass out from lack of oxygen, the sergeant released him.

"Now assume the position."

Buck bent over the desk and let the sergeant batter his hole. He expected it to be unbearable, but it felt good.

"How's that, grunt? Does it make your pussy feel good?"

"Yes."

Bam! Sarge smacked the back of his head. "Yes, what?"

"Sir, yes, sir!"

"That's more like it!" He humped with wild abandon, unmindful of any damage he might be causing. Buck was surprised at how little it hurt this time. His hips began to quiver. The quaking movement passed up his abdomen and down his thighs. He moaned softly. Something good was happening, really good. Staring face down at the desk, he let a little drool drip onto the ink blotter. He was in an altered state. His hips bucked and thrust involuntarily.

"Sir, what's happening?"

Sarge spanked Buck hard. "You're coming like a woman, that's what. Keep it up. Feels good on my cock."

Buck didn't have a choice. He spasmed and shivered, sailing on a wave of bliss unlike any he'd felt so far. His eyes fluttered, and he laid his head on the desk.

"Don't pass out on me, boy!" The sergeant gave a cruel slap to Buck's fat buttocks. His head remained on the desk, but he moaned to let his impaler know he was still with him, albeit in a parallel dimension.

"You ready for my cum, boy?"

Buck nodded, his chin rustling on the soft blotter paper.

"Yeah? Yeah!" Sarge was close. Buck could feel the rhythm change as his drill instructor raced toward orgasm. Without warning, the rhythm passed from the commanding officer to the grunt. Buck felt sperm building in his balls.

"Oh, yeah! Take it!" The sergeant unleashed a torrent of cum in Buck's guts.

Buck couldn't stop the white tide from flooding out of him, even if he wanted to. His dick, trapped by the desk, spurted hot cum down the sides and onto the carpet.

The sergeant zipped up his pants. Buck scanned the room for a paper towel or something to clean up his mess. "Get out. I'll clean up your mess."

9

ALOYSIUS AND HIS BIG MOUTH

Buck limped back to his bunk. Two grunts from his squad were standing next to Aloysisus. "Hey there, Buckie!" A big grin crossed his face.

Buck frowned. "Uh, hi. What's up?"

Aloysius leaned forward in a conspiratorial whisper. "This is Dave and Enoch. I told 'em what you can do."

Buck felt his stomach drop. He had his hands full with the sergeant already. "Uh, you did?"

Aloysius and his two buddies nodded. Dave was tall, skinny, and pimply, with brown eyes and jet-black hair growing out from his shaved head. Enoch was broad-shouldered and about the same height as Buck. He had pale blue eyes and a reddish-blond dusting of hair sprouting from his scalp. Buck sized them up. He couldn't see what Dave was packing, but Enoch had a noticeable bulge. Buck felt his heart race as he dealt with his conflicting feelings.

On one hand, he was stretched, used, abused, and worn out from his latest session with Sarge. On the other hand, he felt a deep, animal desire — a perverse need to satisfy these men in whatever way they wanted. He felt his cock grow heavy in his pants.

Dave leaned and said, "We was gonna fuck ya if you

let us." He wasn't too bright. Buck hid his annoyance at having the obvious explained to him.

His mind said, "No," but his dick spoke. "Yeah, okay. There's an empty Quonset hut out back. Meet me there."

Buck hadn't expected Aloysius to join the two men, so he was surprised to see all three men. His guts churned a little, thinking about Aloysius's cock. It wasn't as big as Sarge, but it was still pretty brutal, mainly because the dumb hick didn't know much about fucking.

Wordlessly, the three men stripped. Enoch had trouble pulling out his fatigues. His pink cock was long and fat. It bobbed in the air like a seagull looking for crumbs. Buck heaved a sigh of relief when he saw Dave's average soft cock. Then he groaned when he saw it swelling and lengthening out of all proportion to its size. In less than a minute, it was bigger than Enoch's. Then there was Aloysius, barely five feet tall and mostly dick. Buck felt dread and anticipation in equal measure. He was hopelessly addicted to cock. The two new men gasped as he stripped off his fatigues, revealing his wide monster.

Aloysius chuckled. "Don't worry. He's not gonna fuck you. He likes it in the ass."

Buck reddened when he heard his sexuality reduced to six words, but deep down, he knew it was true. He loved getting it in the ass. He yearned to fuck someone, but he was okay if he didn't. His ass was a pussy now. He had a fuckstick in front and a dickhole in back. All of it was great.

Enoch pulled a cord from his pocket, grabbed Buck's wrists, and bound him to a bed frame.

"What's that for?"

Enoch said, "That's how my Daddy did it. So's we wouldn't touch him none. Bible says touching your daddy's a sin."

Buck wanted to protest, but having his hands tied made his dick get even harder. His ass was still slippery with Sarge's cum and Vaseline.

Dave plunged into Buck until his head thumped his kidneys. It didn't hurt after Sarge.

"Goddamn, he's loose."

Aloysius hopped from one foot to another. "I told you. Like a cow pussy, right?"

Dave shrugged. "Yeah, I reckon so."

Enoch said, "You're sick. Cows are for eatin'."

Buck marveled that the IQs of these three men probably didn't add together to his. Dave fucked hard, punching Buck's rectum ineptly. "He ain't deep enough."

Buck twisted to let Dave in. The cock sailed past the gaping junction and into his colon. The sergeant had forged a tunnel that was wider than Dave. Only at the rectum and the inner junction did Buck's insides clasp onto Dave's mighty cock. But it was enough. The young stud snorted and humped faster and faster before holding still.

"Oh, shit, here it comes." And it did. Dave coated Buck's already slick guts in a new layer of dick frosting. Dave's cock deflated so fast it caused Buck to cramp. He pulled it out like a wet balloon.

Enoch stepped behind Buck, his angry pink cock throbbing. He held Buck's forehead, pulling his head back, using it as leverage as he forced his way in. Enoch's dad must have been pretty hung because Enoch knew all about the inner junction. He went right in to the hilt. Buck barely felt the massive cock as it sailed in and out. The way Enoch grasped his head was annoying initially but gradually turned him on. He'd never been fucked in such a helpless position. He saw from the corner of his eye as Dave slipped out the doorway. It was close to lights out, and Buck had Aloysius still to serve.

Blessed with youth, Enoch erupted after only a few minutes. It went on for a minute or more. When he pulled out his throbbing member, it dragged a waterfall of semen with it. As the slippery spunk hit the floor, it sounded like a clogged gutter splattering onto the bare concrete on a rainy day.

Enoch stood back, watching Aloysius. He jacked off casually, maybe thinking he had time for another. Buck wasn't sure what was going through his mind. As Aloysius entered, he felt the first pain since Sarge. The little guy was too damn thick.

"Ow, fuck, Al, go slower!"

Aloysius snickered. "Sorry, man. I thought you was all loosed up by now."

Buck ignored the atrocious grammar. His bunkmate was cruel, stabbing him with his flesh sword in grunts and slaps. Unlike the other two men, Aloysius took a long time. Buck relaxed and felt that throbbing wave build in his hips. He bucked, orgasming in his ass again. What Aloysius lacked in brains, he made up in technique. He was a fast study. As Buck's bottom quivered, Aloysius whistled. "I'm doing that, ain't I?"

Buck nodded.

"Well shit, then, let me do it some more. That feels real fuckin' good."

Whatever combination of moves made Buck quake, Aloysius had it figured out. He kept doing it, and Buck's legs nearly collapsed. He'd probably have hit the ground if his wrists weren't tied to the bunk. Enoch shot his wad again, then left.

As his bunkmate sped up, Buck heard footfalls. He turned to see Dave leading two guys from a different squad. They watched, holding their crotches and rubbing themselves hard. Aloysius loved being on stage. He lifted one arm like a bull rider, thrusting and pumping Buck's backside like a rodeo star.

"Watch and weep, boys!" Aloysius took extremely

long strokes, exposing the head and then plunging to the hilt.

One of the new guys said, "Holy fuck, that little guy's huge!"

His friend said, "So's that dude," pointing to Buck.

Aloysius held Buck's waist, and jackrabbited hard. The friction made the sound of a fist smacking into a palm. Then he stopped short, holding Buck's ass against his hips.

"Aw, yeah!" He gave Buck a new coat of paint in his colon.

Enoch returned with two more men, both rubbing their crotches. Word was spreading. Buck wasn't going to get any sleep tonight. One by one, the young grunts stepped up and unloaded inside Buck. He lost count. About an hour before sunrise, someone cut him loose and walked him back to his bunk, where he collapsed, a huge grin spread from ear to ear. He fell asleep as cum leaked out of his ass, soiling his sheets.

At reveille, Buck was too exhausted to get out of bed. Sarge yanked him out of the bed, revealing the massive cum stain.

"What's this, Grunt?" His whisper quivered with a barely suppressed rage.

Buck said, "It's all you."

Sarge smacked him. "Come to my office."

He slammed the door and turned to Buck. "I told you that first night you were all mine."

Buck nodded. "Oh, okay, sir. I didn't know it was more than just that night, sir."

Sarge's eyes became narrow slits. "You can't fuck with a fucker. You knew better. But I'll give you the benefit of the doubt just this once. From now on, the only cock that goes in your hole is mine."

Buck kept his gaze on his shoes. He didn't want to see the sergeant's angry face. He felt lower than a dog who displeased his owner.

Sarge smacked his hand on the desk. "Assume the position, grunt!"

10

THE WHORE OF FORT KNOX

Word of Buck's generous hole spread throughout the platoon and beyond. When he finished a session with Sarge, the men lined up, waiting to sneak a dick into his hole. Buck loved the attention. He had learned to forego ejaculating in favor of those strange, throbbing orgasms in his guts. He left plenty of his cum on the floor each night, but it came naturally without him touching himself. Much of it was the clear pre-cum that the many cocks drained from his prostate.

With Sarge, Buck had to stroke his ego by shooting his load every time. The sergeant wouldn't come until he did. The other grunts didn't care. They were too focused on splattering his insides with their baby gravy. Most guys were so small that Buck could barely feel them. His favorites were the long, fat ones that squeezed his prostate and stretched his inner hole, leaving their seed in his colon. He also liked the short fat cocks, because they milked him like a cow. The pressure on his prostate was constant.

Buck learned to go to the head before climbing into bed. That way, the Sarge wouldn't see any evidence of the shenanigans that went on nightly. He was exhausted every morning, but his body adapted. He

found time to catch naps between drills. On week-
ends, he took a hike to the woods, where Enoch
would strap him to a tree. The men would come one
after another, leaving Buck a dripping, quivering mess.
The rough bark against his cock was painful at first,
but he learned to love it. Serving so many men was
hard on Buck's asshole. He got complaints from the
small-to-average guys. Their little penises were no
match for Buck's gaping hole. He blew a few of them,
but the rest turned to each other to get off. Buck
could take any size, but he could only truly satisfy the
big boys. And satisfying them was like a drug to him.
He was strung out on pleasure, cum, and throbbing
cocks.

One Saturday in the woods, Sergeant Dixon stumbled upon the orgy. Buck had seen him angry, but this
was beyond rage. His face turned crimson as he
shouted, "You motherfuckers! Get your fuckin' paws
offa my boy!" The men pulled up their fatigues and ran.
In seconds, Sarge and Buck were alone in the woods.

Buck prayed that Sarge would see that he was tied
to the tree and forgive him. He saw, but he didn't grant
him a pardon.

"You little fucking slut! You know the rules."

Buck tried to wriggle out of it. "Sarge, sir, they
jumped me and tied me up."

The drill instructor held Buck's chin and squeezed
until it hurt. "I saw that fucking smile on your face, you
little faggot. You were willing. That was all you. You're
just a trash bag for other men's cum. You disgust me!"

Buck whimpered when he saw the sergeant pull out
his cruel, knee-length cock. "Take your punishment,
you goddamn faggot!"

Sarge was brutal. He fucked so hard the other men's
cum frothed and fell from Buck's hole. Each time another foamy load popped out, Sarge punched Buck in
the back of the head. Buck saw stars and blacked out.

When he awoke, he was on the doctor's table. His guts were sore. The doctor shook his head.

"You should do what your drill instructor tells you, young man. Now look at the mess. I had to call a specialist, and now they're asking for names. They're asking who did this to you."

Buck shrugged. "I'll tell them."

A military policeman knocked on the door. "May I come in? I need to take the victim's statement."

Buck felt a warm rush as the doctor added something to his drip. As the lights faded, he heard the doctor say, "I'm sorry, but the patient is coming in and out of consciousness. You'll have to come back."

DISCHARGED

When Buck awoke, he was astonished to find a handcuff on his wrist. A nurse came in.

Buck smiled, holding his trapped wrist aloft. "What's this about?"

The nurse frowned. "The doctor told me what you were doing. You should be ashamed."

As the story unfolded in bits and pieces from the various visitors to his room, Buck discovered he was the victim of a smear campaign. The sergeant told the MPs that Buck had 'seduced' his entire squad and the rest of the platoon. Buck was to blame. The men who fucked him were helpless victims of his beguiling wiles. Sarge had "negotiated" on his behalf. Buck had a choice: a trial or a dishonorable discharge. The prosecution would drag Buck's name through the mud. The discharge was a quiet, anonymous alternative.

Buck's fury rose every time he heard the sergeant talking with the doctor in the hall. He wanted to murder him but didn't want to rot for the rest of his life in prison or die in the electric chair. So Buck swallowed his pride, anger, and self-respect and opted for the discharge.

Buck found himself at the Fort Knox bus station with nothing but twenty dollars to his name. He didn't want to call home and explain his predicament to his parents. He was sure there would be questions he was entirely unprepared to answer. No, Buck needed money, shelter, bus fare, anything he could manage. Twenty dollars wouldn't suffice.

Holding his head in his hands, he felt a comforting hand on his shoulder. He lifted his heavy head and stared into the hungry eyes of an overweight businessman.

"What's the matter, son? You look like you're hauntin' a house."

Buck chuckled. "Yeah, I guess I'm pretty near doin' just that."

The businessman's grin was familiar. Buck knew when the man subtly licked his lips that an opportunity awaited.

The businessman nodded in the direction of the restroom. Buck shrugged.

The heavy man pulled Buck into a booth in the bathroom and locked the door. He whispered, "Let me see what you got. I'm greased up and ready."

Buck doubted the man would want him to fuck him once he saw his fat football of a dick. But he was willing to go through the motions. The businessman dropped his trousers, revealing an empty pair of briefs. When he pulled them over his fat thighs, Buck couldn't see his dick. It was trapped in there somewhere. Buried.

There was a note of desperation in the man's voice as he said, "Show me what you got."

Buck felt turned on by this effeminate man with a penis so small he couldn't see it. Something was intriguing about it. Like he was the opposite of Sarge. Instead of being big and brutal, he was soft and tiny. Buck felt an urge to hold the man in his arms. He put the man's head on his shoulder and patted his hair.

"I wanna see your dick."

Buck pulled away and nodded, unbuttoning his

jeans. His cock strained against his boxers as he pulled them down. When his thick dick popped out, the man gasped. Instead of horror or fear, there was an intense desire. He grabbed it, his fingers unable to encircle it in the middle, so he slid down to the base, where his thumb and forefinger almost touched. He tugged a few times, bringing Buck to full mast.

"Oh, God, I want it so bad." The businessman turned to face the toilet and bent over it, spreading his chunky butt cheeks to reveal his hole. It glistened with baby oil or some other grease.

Buck said, "Are you sure you want it? It's gonna hurt."

The man hissed, "Just fuck me. I'll give you fifty bucks."

Buck pushed against the hole, expecting it to put up resistance. It didn't. In one quick movement, his cock pushed through, the widest part passing the sphincter like a hot knife through butter. Buck barely had to turn a corner; the man was so well-worn. Buck felt a moment of disgust until he realized that his ass was probably the same now. He also liked the man's big soft body and fat butt. He didn't mind the rolls of fat. They gave him something to hang onto while he slid quickly through the tunnel.

"Oh, yeah!" The businessman shivered and shook. Buck could see ripples in the flesh. It was hot. He got so hard that he scraped hard against the man's narrow passages. He felt something building.

"I think I'm gonna come."

The man wriggled with anticipation. "Yes, yes! Come in me!"

Buck gave himself over to an involuntary rutting instinct. His hips rocketed back and forth. Each impact against the man's massive behind made the flesh shake. It felt good rubbing against Buck's cock. His balls drew up. He grabbed the man's waist and held himself inside.

"Oh, fuck! Here it comes!"

Buck filled the man with cum. The rotund tore off a piece of a newspaper to soak up the cum, then handed it to Buck, who tore another piece and wiped himself clean.

"Bus to Chicago, boarding now. Five-minute warning."

Buck took his fifty dollars, and with a quick good-bye, he rushed to the ticket booth.

EPILOGUE - BIG HOLE RIVER

When Buck boarded the bus, he realized he was still clutching the newspaper. He had nothing in his nap sack to read, so he opened it up. It was the Helena Independent Record. His eyes landed on the Help Wanted section. An advertisement caught his eye.

"Rugged men needed on Cock's Crow Horse Ranch in Big Hole River Valley. Bunkhouse and meals. Inquire at ANaconda 3-5685"

Buck couldn't face his parents. This remote bunkhouse in the wilds of Montana sounded like the perfect place to escape his guilt and shame. He folded the paper to the ad, determined to call when he got to Chicago. As the bus rolled down the highway, he drifted off to sleep.

II

THE ANACONDA COPPER

INTRODUCTION

The life of a small-town sheriff is difficult for different reasons than that of a big-city cop. In small townships, the sheriff often becomes the factotum. He may moonlight as a mechanic or run a general store. His budget comes from county taxes, which fall short. He may need to repair the brakes on his cruiser and replace missing letters in the office typewriter. He doesn't do it for the love of money; he must love the law and the people of the town he has sworn to protect.

Autonomy and power are perks of the job. Most sheriffs will not abuse this privilege, but there are temptations. Autonomy allows the sheriff to budget his time as he sees fit. He makes his own schedule. Far more dangerous is the power he has over the lives of his citizens. Strong morals must prevail over temptation, be it greed, envy, lust, or any other sin. This story concerns a sheriff who struggles to balance his sense of right and wrong with his primal urges. His morals are his own, but you must judge if they are virtuous or sinful.

BEN DEASY

Anaconda, Montana, situated north of the Big Hole River Valley, is a small town with big-town problems. Copper is the industry that attracted and sustained a population of over 15,000 souls. The Anaconda Reduction Plant, also known as "The Stack," dominates the town with its 550-foot brick smokestack, the tallest masonry structure in the world. The 3,000 men working at The Stack process over 8,000 tons of rock daily, separating slag from copper ore. The other 12,000 citizens of Anaconda are wives, small business owners, store workers, city employees, school children, and a handful of unemployed bums.

Sheriff Whelan 'Stack' Dowd had the dubious honor of maintaining law and order in Anaconda and the rest of Deer Lodge County. His deputy Preston Twomey left during the winter, so he was riding solo for now.

Sheriff Dowd's nickname was given to him in high school when the other players on the football team first saw his soft cock in the showers. He couldn't shake the name "Stack" even after his Dad died from metal fume fever working at the Anaconda Reduction Works. Whenever he heard his nickname, it ate away at a part of his soul. Throughout high school and into his early twenties, his cock continued to grow far beyond the limits of normal male anatomy. Women were fascinated by his legendary appendage. He tried twice to have sex with eager ladies but sent both women to the hospital with damaged cervixes. Then he gave up sex. Well, at least sex with women. His hand became his mistress for ten years.

Then, he started working with Deputy Preston Twomey. Preston showed him that not only could he bring pleasure to himself alone, but he could also jerk off with a good friend. Then he taught Sheriff Dowd that he could fuck a man without damaging him. The largest city in Montana, Great Falls, needed a deputy, and the position paid well. Preston left Stack alone to uphold the law in Anaconda. With Preston gone, Stack needed someone to jerk off with and someone to fuck. He hated his abnormally large genitals, but it was how God built him, and he needed more than a lonely night of masturbation by himself.

In a small town, a man's reputation is common knowledge. Just as the whole town knew that Reverend McNinch hit the bottle, so too did they know that Whelan Dowd earned his nickname "Stack" because of his monstrous appendage. They also knew how he put two women in the hospital and could not find a wife who would risk her life with him, though they never spoke of it. They didn't know about the arrangement between Sheriff Dowd and Preston Twomey or the sinful sex they had. He intended to keep his secret forever. Sodomy is a crime, and he was sworn to uphold the law.

Thinking about his predicament, Stack sat in the station and rubbed his long, thick appendage through his khaki polyester pant leg. It was late, and he needed to close up. He sighed.

The station phone rang.

"Hello?"

"Stack, that you?" It was Dixon Hand, an old teammate.

"Yeah, what's going on, Dix?"

"I saw a guy bust into the Midtown Variety just now. He's still in there."

"Did you get a description?"

"It was pretty dark. He had cowboy boots. Maybe 6 feet tall."

"Thanks, Dix. I'll get over there right now."

Stack checked his holster, grabbed his jacket and cap, and jumped in the cruiser.

Stack owned Midtown Variety. He had hired a great manager, so he got to reap profits as an absentee boss. If somebody wanted to steal from him, they had no idea what kind of hell they faced. Stack turned off his car lights and coasted to a stop. He could see movement inside the store. Parked out back, there was a Buick with Idaho plates. This guy was a stranger.

With his gun drawn, Stack tiptoed into the store. He followed the noise to the pharmacy, where the stranger checked bottles with a flashlight and dropped them into a burlap sack. Stack threw the light switch.

"Freeze! Down on the ground!"

The thief yelped and dropped to the floor. "Don't shoot!"

Stack knelt on the young man's back and cuffed him before hauling him to his feet.

"Sir, I can explain," he said.

"Yeah, so can I. You're a fucking thief, and I caught you."

Stack took the burlap bag and checked the contents. Most of the drugs were familiar to him. He recognized Morphine and Methaqualone, or quaaludes. There were several bottles of heart medicine called Amyl Nitrate—an unusual stash.

"Quite a party you have planned here, son."

"Please, Officer, they're for my mother. She got the

cancer, and now that she can't work, we can't afford no doctor."

"You know how to tell when a thief is lying? His lips are moving."

This young man had a beat-up Buick, dressed like a cowboy, and smelled of 4711 cologne.

Buck took the thief's wallet and examined the driver's license. He was only 19. So young to get mixed up with drugs.

"Ben Deasy of Coeur d'Alene, Idaho, you are under arrest for Breaking & Entering and Larceny."

Ben hung his head, a few tear drops landing on the hard linoleum. Stack felt terrible for the kid. He wasn't a violent criminal; quite the opposite. He was compliant and polite. While Ben's head was hanging, he stole glances at Stack's pant leg.

"What are you looking at?"

"I don't know, sir. I'm not sure I believe what I'm seeing."

"It's a wallet in my front pocket, you queer." Stack had never needed to lie because nobody ever spoke of his deformity. It felt vile to lie.

"If you say so, sir." Ben stared without shame, studying the contours of what was obviously not a wallet.

Then Stack lost control. This young man was fascinated with his cock. This kid wasn't ashamed to stare. Appreciation for his size was a turn-on. He got an erection.

Ben's eyes widened in awe as the long, thick lump in Stack's pants swelled and stretched towards his knee.

Stack interrogated the kid, "What do you need Quaaludes for, anyway?"

"They make sex feel better, sir."

"Better how?"

"Well, um, everything feels tingly, and you relax."

"Relax."

"Yeah, in fact, sometimes you can't get hard."

Stack was genuinely puzzled. A drug that makes your dick limp didn't sound like an improvement to him. "And heart medicine? You said your Mom has cancer. Why heart medicine?"

"Amyl Nitrate is for, um, men who...need to relax certain muscles to enjoy sex. The morphine really is for my mother. I don't do that stuff."

"Your mom with cancer is going to miss you when you're behind bars. Why all the sex drugs?"

"Sir, she only has a few weeks left. I was stupid to try this."

"I get it, but why the-"

"Sex helps me forget my pain and the drugs make sex painless."

Suddenly, Stack put the pieces together. This boy, Ben, was like Preston—a passive homosexual.

Desperation brought Ben Deasy to Anaconda. Stack felt desperate. He knew right and wrong. He knew moral gray areas, too.

"Ben, I don't know if your mother is sick or if you're a dope fiend. If she is sick, she needs two or three months' worth of morphine."

"That's all I took." He pointed to the shelf. Sure enough, there was much more left untouched. In his bag were just a few cases and a box of hypos.

"Let me see your arms."

Ben's arms were clean. Not so much as a pinprick. Fuck. He knew taking the law into his own hands was immoral, but this kid needed to get home to his mother.

"Morphine is schedule 1, Ben. Do you know what that means?"

"A longer jail sentence?"

"Correct. So it's a good thing your mother had a prescription. You lost it, but we can look the other way this time. Right?"

Ben nodded.

"Methaqualone is not scheduled. Stealing it is a crime, but it's just a misdemeanor. Amyl Nitrate isn't even on my radar. What do we do?"

Ben's tears slowed. He saw salvation.

The sheriff said, "Let's put them back, shall we?"

Stack restocked the shelves, leaving one bottle of Amyl Nitrate and one bottle of quaaludes on the pharmacy counter.

"I need to write a report, and I may need your help filling in some gaps. Will you follow me to the station?"

Ben Deasy of Coeur d'Alene, Idaho, was a kid who made a dumb mistake. He was also brave to tell as much as he did. At the station, Stack filed a statement with some truth to it, leaving out other details that would incriminate both of them.

When Stack stepped out from behind the desk, revealing the outline of his huge penis, Ben got very brave.

"Sir, I am so grateful. I want to show my appreciation."

Stack passed him the two bottles he nicked at the Midtown Variety. "You're gonna need these, son."

Two quaaludes and twenty minutes put Ben in a talkative state.

"Please, Sheriff, can we do it in the cell?"

The thin mattress was the same one where Stack learned how to fuck Preston. He remembered how much pain the Deputy endured until repetition and an extra large tub of petroleum jelly got him loose enough to take him. Quaaludes and Amyl Nitrate would have saved a lot of time.

Ben lay on his back, knees near his ears. Stack oiled his ass with Vaseline. While his thick finger was inside the boy, he heard a quick intake of breath, then a loosening. Ben had just inhaled Amyl. Two fingers, then three, and the hole just kept stretching.

Ben's pink hole still looked too small for Stack to fit.

"Sheriff Dowd, I wanna see your cock. Why you hidin' it?"

The kid was loopy, harmless, and horny.

Stack sighed. He knew there was a good chance that once Ben saw what he was in for, it would send him running.

"Before I show it, you know you don't have to do this, right?"

"Are you kidding? I have never wanted anything so bad in my life!"

Stack took off his shirt, revealing a muscular, V-shaped torso. Ben reached up and touched his navel, tracing a line of hair that led to his crotch.

"Oh god! Just touching you feels so good, Sheriff!" It was the quaaludes talking. What happened next was where the rubber met the road.

Stack unbuckled his tight polyester khakis. He was stuck in them, as often happened. His stiff cock made removing them a real chore. He struggled until the pants were halfway to his knees. They bunched up around his giant head.

"Let me help." Ben's tiny fingers were able to un-wrinkle the legs, and suddenly, Stack's semi-hard cock swung free. It slapped Ben with an uppercut as it stood tall.

"Jesus Christ! That's not possible! It has to be the biggest dick in the West!"

Stack grinned. The boy wasn't scared, just apprecia-tive. "It's not hard yet. Can you help?" Stack lifted the end of his cock to Ben's mouth.

"It gets bigger?" Ben greedily tried to put the head in his mouth, but it wouldn't fit. He had to hold the length of the massive cock with two hands spaced apart, like a suspension bridge. He did his very best to get it in his mouth, but he ended up licking it like an ice cream cone.

This felt good. Stack hardened, swelling thicker still and long enough that he had to step back so Ben could move without hitting his head on the cell wall.

Rock hard now, Stack reclaimed his cock head from Ben's mouth. He gave his monster a liberal coating of Vaseline then pressed the head against the young man's anus.

Ben shivered with pleasure, not fear. The 'ludes intensified nerve sensations. He lifted the bottle to his nose.

As he inhaled, Stack felt the opening grow wider. He pushed in as gently as he could. Ben continued to breathe the fumes as Stack pressed in. Ben moaned. He put a foot against Stack's hip to stop his push forward. After a few moments, Ben pulled his foot closer, allowing Stack to hit the rear of the anal canal. Ben inhaled again; an opening allowed Stack to move into the colon.

From there, it was a rapid slide all the way in. Stack's hips met Ben's ass cheeks, and his huge balls (which appeared small next to his dick) banged into Ben's backside. Ben wriggled and groaned.

"Sheriff Dowd, you're in me! Here." He handed the bottle to Stack. Stack looked for a place to set it down, but Ben pushed the bottle to his nose. Suddenly, the whole world went white. The throbbing in Stack's head matched the intense pulse of his dick.

Ben said, "Oh god, it feels like a living animal is inside me. It's moving on its own."

Stack took another long whiff, then started fucking the little guy. He pounded the depths but didn't take long strokes. He liked the feeling of Ben's colon sphincter massaging the first few inches of his dick. He wasn't sure he could get back in that deep if it popped out. Missing the opening with a hard pound in the wrong place could put the kid in the hospital.

Ben sensed Stack's reticence. He snatched the

bottle of Amyl Nitrate. "You can fuck me all the way in and out if I have this."

Ben was right. Stack took long strokes and found his way past the barrier with ease. He hadn't been able to do this with Preston. It was a sensual pleasure unlike any he had known. This young man was talented. With a lift and swing of his legs, he came onto all fours, Stack's humongous cock rotating inside him.

Now, Stack could go even deeper. He pressed his pubic bone into Ben's crack, making skin contact with the hot, moist opening.

Ben was leaking prostate juice from his small limp penis. As Stack pounded harder, the fluid scattered from Ben's soft swinging dick. Hot droplets landed on Stack's leg.

Ben said, "Shit. You're making me cum like a girl! You're turning me into a girl!"

Stack reached down and fingered Ben's penis, which felt and acted like a giant clitoris. As he rubbed it harder, it grew stiff. This turned Stack into a fuck machine. He plunged and pulled the entire length in and out of the stretched hole. One time he pulled too far, and his cock fell out. Stack grew dizzy looking at his work: Ben's hole stayed open, dilated. Stack could see right into Ben's fuck chamber; it pushed him over the edge. He was going to fill that hole with come.

Before Ben could snap shut, Stack rammed his grotesque appendage inside. Ben moaned. Stack's busy fingers trumped the quaaludes, keeping the thief's dick hard. He felt a real orgasm approaching.

With his free hand, Stack touched one of Ben's nipples, and the boy exploded. He shot torrents of cum onto the wool blanket. He quaked, and his legs gave out, leaving him on bent knees. "Oh my god. Oh, dear Lord. Stack, you fucked me so good!"

Stack felt his cock compressed inside Ben with his collapse. It felt terrific. Ben handed the bottle over.

Stack took a whiff, and it sent him into a blind orgasm. As he regained vision and sense, he could feel weeks of cum spewing forth into Ben.

He throbbed out another quarter cup of semen.

He wanted to see the gaping anus his powerful rod created. Still hard, he pulled out fast, causing Ben to jump. With his cock out came a coffee mug's worth of cum. It dripped on the blanket, forming a massive puddle on the cell floor.

Ben's anus was wide open, like a mother crowning at birth. Stack blew air inside while the hole closed. Ben pressed his abdomen and released the air, along with another puddle of semen.

"Sheriff, I have never been fucked like that. I don't think I can make it back to Coeur d'Alene tonight. I'm not sure what to do."

Sheriff Whelan "Stack" Dowd grinned. He locked the boy in the cell.

Ben panicked. "No! You promised!"

"I'll be back to let you out in the morning. I gotta go home,"

"Can I come to your house?"

"No. Stay here until tomorrow."

BUCK HARTIGAN

Stack had broken so many laws he couldn't count them. All that was just to find an accommodating hole to take his gargantuan cock. He saw Ben as a hole. Younger guys like Ben had so little in common with him. Stack let him limp away home on his own recognizance the following day.

The kid had stashed his mother's morphine in his Buick. He forgot his quaaludes and Amyl at the station, so the Sheriff hid them at his house. His lies and secrets forced him into deeper shit.

He went to the Midtown Variety to check on his employees. The store manager, Charlene, was upset about the signs of a break-in.

"He took morphine! We have to report that." She worried too much, so he didn't worry nearly as much.

"Charlene, I got a call last night about this. When I got here, nobody was around. How much morphine did he steal?"

"Well, that's the funny part. He took some sedatives and such and a two-month supply of morphine but left the rest. What kind of junky leaves morphine behind?"

Stack needed to lead her in the right direction.

"Why would someone only need two months when they could have years of it?"

Charlene brightened. "He must be sick. He ain't gonna live two months. Oh, that's so sad." She covered her mouth.

"I filed a report at the station. We should be good."

Later that night, a call came in from Jim Antonik over at The Lucky Lady, one of Anaconda's less reputable bars.

"Stack that you?"

"Who else?"

"Hey, hurry down. Harley Grew is picking a fight with an out-of-towner. Things could get ugly."

Things already were ugly if Harley was involved. He was a short man with a barrel chest, about as tall as he was wide. He looked and sounded like a bullfrog. When he drank, his demons ran the show.

The cruiser pulled up in front of the bar. A circle formed around Harley and a young man with an angelic face. Harley was swinging at the kid, but his short, stumpy arms didn't come close to the boy. Stack blasted the siren. The fight ended.

Stack had no Deputy to play bad cop, so it was all him. "All right. Can someone explain what happened?"

Harley spit in the boy's direction. "That kid is a faggot."

"Are you saying that this handsome young man made a pass at you, Harley?" Stack put the emphasis on 'you.'

The crowd jeered. Stack turned to the stranger.

"Do you find Harley attractive?"

The stranger shook his head.

"What's your name, son?"

"Buck. Buck Hartigan."

"How long you in town?"

"My Trailways bus leaves tomorrow afternoon."

Harley leaped in, "He was making passes at me, Stack."

"That's Sheriff Whelan Dowd to you, Mr. Grew.

Now look, I'm sure this is all just a simple misunderstanding. Judging by the evidence, I'm gonna have to haul you both to jail for assault. Let's go boys." He pushed Buck and his rucksack into the cruiser, but Harley wouldn't budge.

"Do you want me to add resisting arrest to your charges, Harley?"

"You can't make me share a seat with that perverted fag."

Stack stood by the back door of the cruiser. "Follow my lead, kid."

The sheriff knew how to end this. "Harley, I apologize. You got rights. You go back in that bar and find you a nice, pretty lady. Don't fight, and I won't have to arrest you. I'll take this pervert back to the station and book him."

Satisfied, Harley shrugged, and the crowd returned to their cups.

Stack climbed in front. "Buck, where are you staying?"

Buck blushed.

Stack said, "You can sleep in a cell tonight."

"Oh no, Sheriff sir, I start work tomorrow down in the Big Hole River Valley."

"Cock Crow Ranch?"

"Yes, sir. Please don't arrest me. I will do anything."

Power corrupts. He had no plans to arrest the kid for anything. He had nothing on him. As sheriff, it would be wrong to use his power to commit sodomy. But the kid did say "anything."

"I'll let you go in the morning if you can take my cock up your ass."

"You got Vaseline?"

Buck and Stack kissed their way through the empty station, tearing off their shirts in a frenzy. Stack knew he was going to be disappointed. The kid was experienced, but no one could take him the first time. If Ben hadn't been assisted by drugs, he would never have made it through.

Buck, on the other hand, was a lot tougher than Ben from Coeur d'Alene. Stack admired his sculpted chest and thick biceps. One arm bore a tattoo.

"Military, eh?"

Buck nodded but kept his mouth clamped onto Stack's left teat. He sucked like it would give him milk.

Stack was trapped in his uniform, unable to get the tight polyester to budge. His cock had grown fully hard from the moves this young stranger made. Buck kneeled and started to lick the massive appendage through the cloth. His tongue felt good, even through the fabric. Buck yanked down Stack's pants, unleashing the monster. He put the top of the head in his mouth and licked it.

"Don't waste your time, kid. It can't be sucked. Let's get you jellied up."

"Sir, let's make a wager. If I can take your whole dick in my mouth, you'll let me fuck you."

Stack guffawed. "And if you can't?"

"You can fuck me twice."

"Deal." They shook.

Buck loosened his double-jointed jaw, then dislocated it like a snake. He engulfed the head and allowed it to slide to his tonsils. Stack nearly shit himself. The young man started swallowing the head like a cobra eating a rat. Soon, it had made its way past the windpipe, blocking it closed. Buck coughed and pulled back. It hurt his epiglottis when Stack's thick cock pressed hard against it.

"You lose–" Stack didn't get to finish. Instead, he let out a moan. Buck pressed inch after inch of the massive fuck stick into his throat until he reached the short and curlies. He bobbed up and down quickly in long strokes. Every thirty seconds, he pulled the head out and exchanged the air in his lungs, then sent it back down as deep as it could go.

Sheriff Stack's knees were giving way. He had to sit on a bench and lay back. Ass feels good, but a blowjob was something he had never experienced. It was like the softest wet hands were stroking him with saliva along every inch of his four-handed cock. This kid was a miracle.

The newness, excitement, and wetness combined to push Stack over. He wanted to go back, make this last forever, but it was too late. He lunged and thrusted until Buck planted his strong hands on the Sheriff's waist to hold him still. Buck pulled back and grabbed the giant spewing smokestack. It blanketed him in syrupy come. The sheriff gasped for air. His whole body was on fire. Buck cleaned the lawman's cock with his tongue. Each lick made Stack twitch with desire. Buck fumbled his way to the can to clean Stack's dick milk out of his eyes.

When he returned, he smiled and kissed the sheriff. "My turn."

Stack grew pale. He had never, ever taken a cock before. Not even in his mouth. His mind wandered to the stash at his house.

"You don't want to sleep here, Buck. Come stay the night with me."

Stack's one-bedroom cottage smelled of men's cologne, coffee grounds, and bed linens in need of a wash. He had no visitors since Preston left town. He tried to straighten up.

Buck retrieved an empty dish soap bottle from the trash. While Stack popped two quaaludes, Buck rinsed the bottle until no bubbles emerged. He filled it with warm water.

"Come here." Stack joined him in the bathroom. He removed all his clothes.

"Get down on all fours, and raise your ass in the air."

Stack obeyed, but he didn't like being ordered around. Not very much.

Buck tilted the dish bottle and placed the nozzle into Stack's ass. He squeezed, emptying the entire bottle into the lawman.

Stack felt a warm stream that slowly became more painful. His innards were spasming.

"Hold it there."

Buck refilled the bottle while the Sheriff fought off dysentery-like spasms. For one horrible moment, he thought Buck would add another bottle on top of the first.

"Go sit on the toilet and let it out."

The sheriff felt immediate relief as water and chunks of poop blasted their way out. Stack went to flush, but Buck needed to see first.

"I'm ready, kid."

"No, you're not. Back in position." He flushed the smelly mess.

Ass in the air, Buck filled Stack with warm water a second time. This time, it didn't hurt. In fact, it felt good. The spasms in his abdomen, together with the effect of the quaaludes, gave him a semi-hardon.

This time, the water carried only a tiny amount of stool with it.

The third round ran clear.

Buck found Vaseline but also a bottle of mineral oil.

"I'm pretty big, Sheriff, so you'll need both."

How big was the kid? He hadn't even checked. He swallowed hard when he saw the outline in his pants. It was a few inches shorter than his, but at one point on the sizable shaft, the convex cock looked as thick as his own.

Quaaludes took away his fear. He felt his whole body glow when Buck touched his chest, brushing his nipple.

The sheriff lay on his back. His horse cock hung

down like a curtain blocking his anus. Buck lifted it and placed it across one thigh, the head resting on the blanket. Stack's eyes widened when he felt a tongue penetrate his hole. Buck was a master ass eater. Stack felt moisture from his earlier enema trickling down. Buck didn't blink; he moved aside and let the water flow onto the blanket.

"Now you're ready."

Buck rubbed mineral oil into Stack's virgin ass, warming him up with one finger. The sheriff marveled at this young man's skill and dexterity. He didn't notice when a second finger slipped in. But then the fingers separated, stretching his smooth anal ring. The fingers hurt now. But the quaaludes allowed the sheriff to shrug it off and focus on the feeling of being touched so deeply. He relaxed.

The third finger made Stack grab the amyl. Like magic, Buck's painful invasion transformed into a relaxing exercise of his tight muscles.

With oil and jelly on his cock, Buck was ready to take the sheriff in his own bed.

Stack's elephant-like cock slipped between his legs, knocking hard into Buck's growing member. Buck lifted the heavy appendage and wrapped it around the thigh, pinning the head beneath the sheriff's buttocks. He hoped that would prevent further collisions of heavy cockflesh.

Buck pressed his relatively small cockhead against the sheriff's puckered hole. It entered easily, as it always did. As Buck pushed forward, his convex penis began to stretch the sheriff wide. The sheriff squirmed and hollered until Buck picked up the amyl and held it to the man's nose. He forced the thickest middle part past the sphincter so that moving forward caused the hole to close further. Stack's ass swallowed Buck's cock. But it stopped at the end of the rectum. Stack knew what he needed to do. He inhaled deeply from the bottle and shifted sideways. With a pop, the lad's head found its way past the sheriff's inner ring. The thickest part of his cock stopped right there, holding open the tight entryway deep inside.

Quaaludes and Amyl Nitrate were helpful with this ass violation, but they couldn't mask the pain. The sheriff felt every sensation, both good and bad, enhanced by the drugs. He moaned with joy and cried with pain.

Buck withdrew partway, sending a flood of relief to the sheriff. If Buck were to continue pulling out, the thickest part of his cock would stretch the man's anus painfully. Buck knew how to fuck a virgin. He kept the wide part moving up and down the rectum, never exiting and only entering fully for punctuation to his long strokes.

The sheriff was in a heaven he couldn't have imagined a few days ago. This ex-army man, bound for the bunkhouse tomorrow, was a magician with a powerful and agile wand.

The sheriff pinched one of Buck's nipples. The kid slowed his fucking and made the sound of someone enjoying a banana split. He shuddered. If the sheriff kept pinching him, he would blow a load early.

Stack was acclimating to his new passive role. He hefted his unwieldy cock into both hands and pumped up and down. He grew hard, then harder. He bent his neck forward an inch and took part of his head in his mouth. How Buck had managed more than the tip was a true mystery.

Buck pulled out roughly and flipped the sheriff onto his hands and knees. Like a dog, Buck took him from behind. The sheriff felt every inch entering and exiting, stretching him like a rubber band and releasing with each thrust. His giant pudendum hung much like a horse's would. Stack placed his head on the mattress and used both hands to jerk his meat in time with Buck's thrusts.

Tingling from head to toe, Stack could hardly stand the intense pleasure in his nerve endings. Having Buck buried deep inside him made him feel like a woman. It was a narcotic, and he was addicted to cock in his ass. He could never go back to being completely on top now. He needed his ass fucked too. He could be the woman, even with his third leg of a cock getting in the way. With his face buried in the blanket, he couldn't see. It made all the other sensations light up. He had a nice big cock sliding back and forth in his butt while he jerked his own enormous dick. He felt a connection. Buck felt it, too. They were exchanging power. Buck penetrated and dominated the sheriff, who gathered sexual energy from the pleasure of being invaded and stretched. Their breaths were in sync.

At the same instant, each man announced he would come. Buck thrashed wildly inside Stack. The sheriff's tired wrist reached its goal. When he climaxed, he made a white, gooey map of France on his blanket. Buck unleashed cupfuls of hot come up the Sheriff's ass.

Stack felt the flood inside his bowels. It made him come even harder until he had a map of Russia. He suddenly understood why Deputy Preston Twomey had begged for Stack's cum every chance he got. He endured untold suffering so he could feel flooded with the hot syrup of another man's lust for him. He felt withdrawal pains as his anus expelled Buck's softening cock.

Buck loved virgin men. He would have let Stack fuck his ass, but they were both sweaty and tired. They curled up together like two spoons and drifted to sleep.

❦ 3 ❦

LARS JOHNSSON

Neither man knew how to cook much, so Stack drove them to Butte to the Copper Plate for breakfast. He didn't want anyone asking nosy questions about Buck or why he was limping like that.

There was plenty of time to fuck before Buck's Trailways bus left for Big Hole River. Buck insisted Stack should fuck him this time.

Buck was experienced and knew how to control his sphincter to provide more pleasure. He needed no drugs. He's spent his time in the army mostly on his back, taking soldiers of every shape and size. He had never seen anything like Stack's pendulous prick, but he wasn't frightened. Mineral Oil and Vaseline will push a pig through a pinhole.

Stack lubricated himself and the young man. He skipped fingers and put his cockhead right against the supple hole.

"You ready?"

Buck nodded.

Stack pushed his fat cockhead into Buck, who grinned and sighed. Stack was rock hard, as thick and long as he could get. He exerted brute force to enter the rectum, hitting bottom before he was halfway in.

Buck scooted, and Sheriff Dowd's mighty cock pushed past the inner door deep inside.

Buck hadn't felt pain like this since he first learned the joys of anal sex. He was a stoic and let the pain run its course until he was comfortable having Stack's cock fill him completely.

Stack fucked hard, banging away inside his new friend. Buck felt some damage being done, but he didn't care. He had the biggest cock of his life, even bigger than Sarge's, lodged completely inside him. Stack's balls slapped against the young man's butt, making a clapping noise. Buck's sighs became moans. His own sizable rod was stiff and throbbing. Stack twisted a nipple. Buck squirmed and shivered with the added stimulus. His pisshole dribbled with clear semen.

Buck was younger but more experienced than Preston had been. Stack missed his old fuck buddy. He was angry at him for leaving so suddenly. He let some of that anger affect his performance.

Buck didn't complain; he took Stack's full length as it pounded deep inside his left abdomen. The sigmoid moved up and down, bumping into his surrounding organs. Stack was so thick and far up his colon that Buck felt his gut push his kidney. The boy was glad he had cleaned himself thoroughly. Buck sucked in his stomach, revealing the sea monster moving inside him.

Stack couldn't believe his eyes. He put his hand around the lump and squeezed. He was fucking and jerking off at the same time. Then he felt Buck's hands on his nipples, tugging and twisting gently. The added stimulus was like plugging a toaster and a clothes iron into the same outlet; he blew a fuse. He saw spots in front of his eyes. He swooned. To keep from falling, Stack grabbed Buck around the waist and lifted him. The Sheriff lay flat on his back. Buck didn't lose a beat. He squatted and straightened his legs in rapid succession. Stack stayed deep inside him, even when he straightened his legs all the way. There was just so much cock. Buck had been with very big men, but Stack's was in a category of its own: super cock.

The young stud bounced in the prone sheriff's lap and pleasured himself. He reached forward to pinch Stack's nipples again. It was a wonderful experience, but he couldn't take it much longer. After a few minutes of titty twisting, the sheriff's breaths grew shallow. Buck increased the pace of his self-impalement. His fist flew up and down his cock in time with the rhythm of his lap dance.

Stack was going to come. He watched Buck Hartigan bring himself to orgasm in curving arcs of white. It pushed the sheriff over the edge, and he flooded the young man's hole with a load of sticky white semen. They stayed locked together for minutes. Buck stood upright. Stack's softened cock succumbed to gravity. Buck released the humongous tube of flesh. As it exited, Buck cupped his hand to catch the cum. It filled to overflowing. He carefully lifted it to his lips and sipped.

Stack watched in fascination as the boy ate his gravy. When the semen was finished, he leaned forward and deeply kissed the sheriff—the taste of cum mingled in their mouths.

Stack enjoyed being with a younger lover, but he needed the companionship of someone older, like him. He wasn't sad when he put the boy on the Trailways Bus to the Big Hole River Valley. Buck would be living in a bunkhouse with a lot of men. He needed to share his talents with them. If the sheriff wanted to experience a blow job again, he could drive 80 miles and haul the kid in on some false pretext. He waved goodbye, knowing he would see Buck again.

Sheriff Whelan "Stack" Dowd sat on the Trailways bench and fished a Marlboro out of his shirt pocket.

"Need a light?"

It was Lars Johnsson, the bachelor and volunteer

fireman. Lars was one of a handful of Swedes in this town of Irishmen and Indians. He handed Stack a zippo.

"I think they call it irony," the sheriff said.

"How do you mean?"

"Getting a light from a fireman."

Lars chuckled and sat beside Whelan. They had graduated from Anaconda High a

few years apart. Lars migrated from Sweden when he was thirteen. He was older than Stack. He ran track and field. He had gained some weight, but it appeared to be all muscle. His day job at the reduction works kept him active, Stack figured.

"Who was that on the bus?"

Stack hated nosy questions, especially when he couldn't answer honestly. Lies were second nature to him now, but they led to problems.

"My mother's cousin's kid Buck. He's heading off to college in Idaho Falls.

"He looks big for a freshman."

"Oh, he's an early bloomer." Stack cursed himself for letting this lie run away from him. He wanted to shut Lars down.

"He is handsome, too."

Stack took a deep inhale and blew the smoke out.

"How's your mother?"

Lars got a distant look in his eyes. "She's holding on."

"How are you?"

"I am alright. It is hard not having family."

"How do you do it?"

"I'm 17 years sober. I got God and a group of drunks that support me. That is all that matters."

Lars shifted in his seat, adjusting his crotch. Stack saw the outline of a thick Swedish cock along Lars's thigh.

"Sheriff Dowd, do you enjoy living here?"

"Sure, Lars, why?"

"Oh because you see the same faces all the time. I sometimes wonder what it would be like to live in a big city like Great Falls or Boise."

"More faces, more strangers."

Lars nodded. "Still, we got a lot of nice faces here in Anaconda. You have a very nice face, Sheriff."

"Well, thanks, Lars. You have a good face too. It was nice talking with you."

He stubbed out his smoke in the ashtray. Lars put his hand on his thigh as he watched the sheriff stand.

"I would like to talk some more. You got time?"

"Nah, I gotta get back to the station. Thanks for the light."

Getting into his cruiser, Stack cursed under his breath. Lars was ruggedly handsome. It wasn't a sure thing, but he thought the Swede was coming on to him. He was spent from the last 18 hours with Buck. Fuck it. They lived in a town of 15,000 people who all seemed to know each other's business. Not worth the risk.

❦   4   ❦

MAYFIELD PAINE

Stack slept in. His ass hurt from Buck's pounding, and his cock was raw. But he felt better than last night. Before work, he stopped in at Midtown Variety; Charlene had an out-of-town man in her office. She ran to the sheriff.

"Where you been, Whelan? I been calling the station all morning."

"Who's that man? Is he IRS?"

"Shoplifter from Boise. Too embarrassed to pay if you ask me."

She held up the stolen goods. It was a long, slender electric massager.

Stack was intrigued.

"I'll need to book that in as evidence. Let me take him off your hands."

Stack had a lot of power, and he knew it. He wasn't a cruel man, but he had an inner demon who got off on intimidation. He swaggered into the office, closing the door. Up close, the man looked to be about forty. He had a thick mustache, which improved his looks. He was in decent shape under his pearl snaps and cowboy hat. Stack asked for ID.

"So, Mr. ... Mayfield Payne didn't want to pay for this?"

The man reddened.

Stack waited. Nothing. "You think you can waltz into our little town and steal from us?"

"No, sir."

"Is this for your wife?"

"Yeah."

"Bullshit! You ain't got no wedding ring!" Silence.

Stack slammed both hands on the desk. "What's it for?"

"M-m-massage. I gotta bad back."

"I doubt that. You were gonna shove this up your ass."

The man quivered, and a tear fell onto one cheek.

"Am I right? Huh?"

The thief nodded.

"You know what we do with thieving perverts like you?" Mayfield shook his head. It was time to switch to good cop.

"We take you to the station, write a citation, and send you on your way."

"I am so sorry, Sheriff. I can explain."

"I doubt that, but you can finish your confession in the cruiser."

Stack made a big show of dragging his suspect out of the store in handcuffs. It set a good example. He tucked the stolen box under one arm to hide its contents from the customers.

In the cruiser, Mayfield Payne explained his innocence.

"I was here on business with the Reduction Works. I couldn't buy this in Boise; too many people would talk."

Stack listened.

"I left a ten-dollar bill at the register and tried to leave, but that ferocious woman–"

"Charlene."

"Yeah, Charlene, she put me in a headlock. I tried to tell her about the ten-spot, but she wouldn't listen."

"Are you saying I owe you change? That thing is only $3.99."

"I don't need change."

"Why did you want it?"

After a long pause, Mayfield admitted his faults. "I got a tiny dick. Women won't have me. It won't stay in."

Stack felt deep sympathy for the man.

"Physique Pictorial had an article about male anatomy, and it said I could have an orgasm in my ass."

"What about jacking off?"

"Sure, but it gets lonely and boring. So, I tried a few different things. A carrot, a cucumber; I won't ever try a zucchini again."

Stack laughed.

"So, no orgasm?"

"Nope. I thought this could do the trick. I have put objects big and small up there, but they don't do it. I need movement."

"What's the biggest thing you ever put up there?"

"A wine bottle."

"And you didn't ask a man to fuck you?"

"I don't think men would want me. My dick is so small."

"Mayfield! That kind of man would want to fuck an ass, not a dick."

"How do you know? Are you like that?"

They pulled into the station. Sheriff Dowd got out the handcuff keys.

"You want to keep the cuffs on?"

A nod.

When it rains, it pours. Three men in as many days. All strangers, so no strings and no gossip.

"I can take you back to your car and get you your six bucks change, but we gotta wait, so it looks like I booked you."

"I don't have anywhere to be. I can wait." Mayfield raised his cuffs skyward and attached himself to a coat hook. "I'm your prisoner for now."

"Yeah, you are. Before we go further, I should tell you my nickname is Stack."

He pointed towards the window with the view of the tallest brick smokestack in the world. He traced the outline of his soft cock down his pant leg."

"Holy Christ!"

"Yep, you and me got the same problem with women for opposite reasons. I only been with two, and they both went to the hospital."

"It's massive!" Mayfield looked pale like he might faint, but fascination danced in his eyes. Stack stripped the man naked below the waist. His tiny erect penis looked like a flesh thimble.

The sheriff plugged in the stolen device, which came alive in his hands. It vibrated so hard it felt like a mild electric shock. It had no switch; he unplugged it.

"Alright, Payne, is this what you want?"

He nodded. The sheriff found his tub of Vaseline and applied it to the device.

When Mayfield turned toward the wall, he exposed a very loose asshole. Clearly, he had been putting big things in there for a long time now. The lining was open and folded, like a labia majora. The vibrator slipped in quickly. The electric cord dangled from Mayfield like a tail. The Idahoan clamped his buttocks to hold the hole closed, then nodded.

Stack plugged it in. Mayfield's voice went three octaves higher as he shrieked in delight.

"Oh my god! Oh, Jesus! I'm gonna, I'm gonna," and his little penis shot out sperm.

Stack reached to unplug the massager.

"No, wait! I can, I can, aaagh. I can keep going." He held the vibrator tightly between his cheeks, his loose anus flapping with the vibrations. It aroused Stack to look at this man's ass that had stretched into a loose vagina. He didn't want to injure this guy but figured he could jerk one out while he watched. He undid his pants and removed the 'Stack' from his tight khakis.

Mayfield had his head buried in one elbow. His words dissolved into grunts and moans. In another three minutes, his hips bucked.

"I'm coming!" And he shot another load on the wall. "Stack, I need you inside me."

"Man, I will rip you apart."

"The wine bottle was about as thick as what you got there," he shivered with the vibrator's pulse.

"Have you gone past the second hole?"

"The what?"

"There's a second hole inside you. Only really long dicks can reach it. Mine plows past it with inches to spare."

"I can take it." Stack wished he had some amyl for this poor guy. But he learned something new before the fuck ended.

"Shall I unplug?"

"No, leave it in."

Stack was sure that Mayfield was going to get injured. That's one hospital trip he hoped to avoid. But his cock was thinking for him. It wanted to touch those loose pussy lips on the man's ass.

When his grapefruit-sized head made contact, he immediately felt the vibrations, which were much more intense than he had imagined. He pushed past the loose hole and felt the vibrator on the tip of his cock. It was better than sex. He wanted to stay there.

"Keep going!" this mustachioed butt freak from Boise was a little too bossy for Stack's tastes. He wanted to show him what it meant to keep going. Holding tight to the electrical cord, he slid past the vibrator and punched the back wall of Payne's rectum. He expected a shriek, not the soft moan of pleasure.

"Is that it? Are you all the way in?" Mayfield looked behind him and gasped when he saw five inches of exposed flesh. Stack took the moment of astonishment to rape the man's virgin inner hole. Now he heard not one but several shrieks of pain.

"Ow! Fuck! You're hurting me!" Stack sighed and started to pull out.

"I didn't say stop! Where are you going?" Stack rammed himself back in all the way. He couldn't believe this man could take this without chemical assistance.

"Oh, sweet Jesus. Mother of god. You tore me a new pussy!" The man wriggled with joy. The vibrations near the base of Stack's cock were intense. He wasn't going to need much time. Ever the controlling boss, Mayfield said, "Put your hands on my little dick and play with me."

As Stack played with the small appendage, he was reminded of the two times he had fucked women. They each had asked him to play with their clitoris to help bring them to orgasm, but each time, he got only a moment to play before he ripped and bruised their cervix, bringing sex to a very early end with a trip to the hospital.

Fiddling with the man-clitoris on Mayfield was better. It drooled constantly, leaking prostatic fluid forcibly ejected by the massager. His hands grew sticky. Mayfield demanded Stack's hand and licked it clean, then ordered him to play some more. Stack pounded in and out of the older man with abandon. The man was not like many men. His tiny dick and loose flappy anus made him more woman than man. And yet he wore a mustache and spoke in a deep voice most of the time. Stack imagined this might be what it's like to fuck a flat-chested woman.

The friction from Stack's cock had pushed the vibrating appliance to the back wall of the rectum. It would never squeeze through the second door, but it was touching it now.

Stack pulled his cock back so his corona was touching the inner door. The vibrator on the other side sent tingling spasms throughout Stack's body.

Mayfield was past words. He panted and uttered nonsense syllables that expressed the intense pleasure he was feeling. Without warning, his cock shot a third time.

Stack could go for a long time if he planned it right. The vibrator threw any plans for a long fuck in the trash. With the speed of a lightning flash, his cock started spitting vibrating ropes of sperm into Mayfield's colon. The orgasm lasted nearly a minute. Ultimately, the vibrator was too much, and he wanted to pull out, but Mayfield forbade it.

"Stay right there. Don't move. We'll both come again."

He was right. Stack played with Mayfield's tiny dick, but they remained motionless as the vibrations coursed through both their bodies. In three or four minutes, Stack felt another wave approaching. It built slowly, weakening his knees. He stayed embedded in the man as he spewed a second orgasm without any fucking or touching. Stack's male energy at that moment turned Mayfield into a howling woman. He moaned as his itty bitty penis shot its fourth or fifth load of ejaculate onto the wall and floor.

Stack was sheriff, so he didn't obey orders when Mayfield wanted another stand-still orgasm. The vibrations on his cock were unpleasant now. As he pulled out of the man, he yanked on the electrical cord, so the vibrator came partway along with him. Stack stretched Mayfield's cunt-like anus on the way out. The skin looked like a sea creature. There was no sound when his giant head popped out, only a gaping red hole and loose flappy skin. Without warning, a river of semen poured out of the open chasm onto Stack's black boots. He cursed. He uncuffed Mayfield, who removed the sperm and vaseline-covered massager from his ass as if it were a toothpick.

Mayfield crouched naked on the floor and began licking the come from Stack's black boots.

Despite his exhaustion, watching the man lick his boots aroused him. His cock stood away from his body at a 15-degree angle, dripping post-coital semen into Mayfield's hair.

The filthy wall and floor, covered in both men's ejaculate, needed cleaning. Mayfield used his tongue to remove all traces of their sinful union.

Neither man spoke in the cruiser on the way back to the store. They were both stewing in their own complexes. Neither man could be with a woman, and yet Stack was so endowed he made a woman out of every man he fucked.

Mayfield, on the other hand, had no choice but to be a woman. He glared at Stack's massive bulge with envy. Then he thought of the burden of carrying it around, being humiliated; they were very alike in some ways. The only difference was that Stack chose to be a man, but he could be the woman if he wanted to.

Stack dropped the stranger out back and handed him the cardboard box.

"You're gonna need a lot of towels, Mayfield. It turns you into a lawn sprinkler."

GUIDO FACCHINO

As quickly as the flood came, so did it dry up. Nobody new or interesting came to town for weeks. Crime was low. Stack contemplated stealing a massager from his own store but thought better of it. What if he got so he could only come with that thing? He heard of such things. He had to resort to Mother Fist and her five little fingers for release. In his case, it required both fists and ten fingers.

Summer heat peaked in early August; with it came fistfights.

Sheriff Dowd got a call from up at the Stack. A fight broke out between Tad Shortbow, a Nez-Perce Indian, and Cleve Redbird, a Lakota Sioux. They both lived in the trailer park outside of town affectionately called "The Reservation" since all the residents were Indians who came to Anaconda to smelt copper at the Reduction Works.

Cleve Redbird was winkte. He had the body of a man but the soul of a woman. Back on the Sioux reservation, Cleve commanded great respect, but here among two dozen different tribes, he was often considered a faggot whore who shouldn't be seen with men or women. Cleve had great dignity in the face of constant name-calling. Indians from tribes who recognized "two-spirits" protected Cleve. But Nez-Perce slags like Tad Shortbow didn't respect Winkte like Cleve.

Pulling up at the Stack, Sheriff Dowd passed the sign that reminded him of his father's untimely death. It read, "Better To Be Careful Than To Be Crippled." His dad was careful all his life. It was the fumes that killed him. The foreman brought Stack to a changing room shower facility. Inside, the two naked men painted a portrait of justice. Tad lay on the ground, out cold. His face was bruised and bloody. Cleve had the beginnings of a black eye and a bleeding knuckle, but otherwise, he remained untouched. Stack noted with delight that Tad had a tiny penis, and Cleve was well above average. Justice takes many forms. A handful of witnesses watched the scene unfold.

Tad regained consciousness. He was too banged up to get to his feet. He covered himself with a hand. Cleve smiled at the sheriff.

"Cleve, tell me what happened."

"That sonofabitch Tad came at me, so I hit him."

"How many times?"

"As many as he attacked me. Maybe five."

Stack regarded the witnesses. "Is that what happened?"

Heads nodded.

"The fuck it is!" Tad shouted from the shower room floor.

"May I ask your version of events?"

"That cocksucker faggot-"

"Tad, please remember you're talking to the law."

"Okay, that faggot Cleve tried to fuck me in the ass."

Again, the sheriff polled the witnesses. Heads nodded, heads shook. One Lakota man defended Cleve. "Tad dropped the soap, and Cleve teased him. It wasn't no rape."

An Omaha defended Tad. "He hung his dick over Tad's backside when he was bent over."

"Cleve, that isn't a fair fight, is it? Tad could never fight back in that contest."

The whole room erupted in laughter. All except Tad, who got unsteadily to his feet, fists clenched, revealing his shamefully small penis.

"Cover yourselves and come with me."

Tad and Cleve sat in the changing room with Sheriff Dowd between them.

"What's really going on here?"

Cleve spoke first. "Tad don't like Winktes. Not for friends anyways."

Ted's eyes narrowed. "Yeah, that's it."

There was a reason Stack chose the law. He had an intuition that frequently revealed the truth. Right now, his itchy ear told him that there was more below the surface. It had no smell, but it didn't smell right.

"Tad, was that the first time Cleve touched you with his penis?"

Cleve let a giggle escape.

"Yeah, and I was scared he'd try to fuck me."

Cleve said, "Like I fuck you in my trailer every night?"

"Shut up, you filthy whore!"

"Was it Shakespeare who said, 'O what tangled webs we weave when first we practice to deceive'?"

"No. It was Sir Walter Scott." Cleve corrected him.

The sheriff admired this man who walked proudly in the light of day. He was intelligent and brave—a better man than him.

"What's that even supposed to mean?" Tad asked.

Cleve looked the sheriff dead in the eye and said, "If you live a life of lies, you're going to trip over your secrets."

Tad said, "I ain't as strong as you. I can't let no one find out about us. They'll think I'm a queer."

"This is a private conversation," Stack said, "I will leave you two to work this out. Your secret is safe with me." But Cleve's words rang in his ears as he left the bickering lovers.

There were reasons he lied. He was a man of the law, forced to break it. Sodomy was illegal in Montana and nearly everywhere else. Some assholes enforced the law, but Montana has always shown a 'live and let live' tolerance towards folks who were different. Some people knew what happened at the Cock Crow Ranch where Buck made his bed now. They never spoke of it, for if they did, they would have to whisper. Whispering isn't polite, so no one talks about such things. But if a man of the law got found out, it would end his career. That's why he stuck to folks from other places. It kept his deepest secret safe.

Coming down Commercial Avenue, he was passed by a big rig hauling ore at 60 miles per hour in a 35 zone. He flashed his siren and stopped the truck.

Copper ore was the blood that pumped through the heart of Anaconda. Stack knew he shouldn't keep this driver long.

The truck came from the mines in Butte. The driver was from Mediterranean stock, maybe Greek or Italian. He had pale green eyes, olive skin, and curly black hair. He looked to be maybe 25. He wore a panicked expression.

"Sheriff, sir, I'm late. The whole Works could shut down because of me."

"License, please. Is that why you were exceeding the speed limit?"

"Yeah, it was, and I'm awfully sorry. If you follow me to the Stack and write the ticket there, it would keep things flowing."

"Tell you what, Mr...Guido Facchino, I'll do you one better. I just came from the Stack and I need to be at the station. Why don't you drop off your load and come get your license back when you're done."

Guido whispered to himself. His eyes were on Stack's left thigh. He was hypnotized.

The sheriff saw a huge boner tenting in Guido's pants.

"Will that work for you, Guido?"

He snapped out of it. "Yeah, I'll come to the station after."

Mike stopped at home to pick up quaaludes, amyl, and the empty dish bottle. He cleaned himself just in case he needed to be the girl.

Guido rolled up an hour later.

The sheriff was ready for him. He had a book of tickets out on his desk. Guido stood by the sheriff, prepared to give him answers.

It was risky, but Stack decided to chance it. "Mr. Facchino, do you want to avoid this ticket?"

"No, sir. I broke the law; I gotta pay."

"You can pay a lot of different ways." Stack plopped his hand down on his thigh and rubbed it softly.

"Officer, I'm not gonna lie. I see your big cazzo in your pants. I got a big one, too."

Guido outlined his long thick cock.

"But I can't pay you that way. I'm too tight."

"Sounds like you tried before."

"I got a tight one. I might be seeing things, but it looks like you got a telephone pole in your pants. Please don't fuck me."

"Guido, you're in luck. I just washed out my ass, and if you agree, you can pay me in sperm up my ass."

Twenty minutes later, Stack was flat on his back in a jail cell, his legs pointing skyward. He was coming on to the ludes, and his bottle of amyl was in hand.

Guido had a big fat cock. It was thick, long, and hard as a rock. A wide vein ran along the underside.

A few minutes earlier, the sheriff had to catch

Guido when he swooned at the sight of Stack's impossibly large soft dick. It had so much power that it caused men to tremble. The sheriff liked the law, but he preferred the power he had over people. His dick was one more way he controlled men.

Now Guido's throbbing cock was pushed up against the sheriff's quivering hole. Stack drew a long breath from the bottle and nodded. Guido leaned forward, sliding effortlessly into Stack. He stretched his rectum with his thick cock. It was long but not long enough to pay a visit to the inner room.

Guido stroked the sheriff's semi-hard cock while he pounded his hole. If he timed it right, it felt like he had a humongous cock, and he was jerking himself off.

Stack inhaled again, giving Guido even more room to hump him. The drugs made him feel electric. His nerves were ablaze with ecstasy. He grew harder as Guido stroked him inside and out. Three weeks with no orgasm made it easier to stay hard.

Guido marveled at the log of flesh in his hands. Two hands full, and the Dick could easily have two more on it and still show some skin. The sheriff was a natural wonder. But Guido pretended this was his dick now. He pointed it like a gun at the Sheriff, at himself, in the air. He didn't have to bend to put the giant cockhead against his face. He licked it like a meat lollipop.

Stack watched Guido worship his manhood. He got more aroused, seeing his huge cock take over the man's thoughts so completely. Guido fucked well, but his mind was focused on the totem before him. Stack knew better than to interrupt, so he pinched his nipples. The ludes acted to separate sensations, and it felt like a third party was there pleasuring his breasts. Combined with a thoroughly stretched hole and Guido's voracious tongue on his cock head, the Sheriff started to feel a pent-up orgasm pushing its way out of his mighty balls. Clear fluid emerged from the piss slit; Guido lapped it up greedily.

Guido was so deep in worship that only the salty taste brought him back in his body. His cock felt wonderful, stuffed up inside the lawman. So wonderful, in fact, that his balls started tingling. He was going to come soon. He put his mouth over Stack's pee hole. He couldn't put the head in, but he could cover the end.

Twisting his own titties put Stack past the finish line. Giant globs of sperm shot out of him into Guido's mouth. The sperm kept coming. It filled Guido's mouth and squirted out the sides, sprinkling a white rain onto Stack's belly and chest.

Guido swallowed what he could and let the rest drip out of his mouth onto the top of Stack's colossal cock. It balanced there, like a partially melted soft serve cone, then cascaded down one side and puddled in the sheriff's pubes.

Guido released his big Italian payload into Stack. His cock was so thick that Stack needed to take another sniff to accommodate the pounding swell of his climax. Stack felt warm cum leak into the second room; Guido's cock was so thick, there was nowhere else for it to go.

Guido didn't go soft. He was stuck like a tight cork inside the sheriff. This happened to him with men. He had a dirty trick he used. Without permission, Guido relaxed his bladder and pissed inside the sheriff. It created pressure in all directions. Some of it entered Stack's colon, but most of it filled the rectum, forcing Guido's cock out through displacement.

If the sheriff weren't so high, he would be angry. Instead, he just imagined that Guido had filled him with the biggest load of sperm on earth. It was so warm it soothed his insides.

Guido finished pissing and popped his dick out. The sheriff was glad the jail cell had a toilet beside the bed.

He was cramping. In one movement, he rolled off the bed onto the john. As was his custom, Stack held his cock up and laid it across his thigh. With waves of pleasurable relief, the sperm and urine cocktail gushed from Stack's ass.

Guido stood dumbfounded. The sheriff had been using this technique to keep his dick dry all his life, but Guido had never seen a man hold it up and lay it on his leg. He started to get hard again. A huge cock affects every man who beholds it. Some get angry and envious. Some lose their balance with rubbery legs. Some get an instant erection. Guido fell into the third category. Huge dicks excited him. He wasn't a fag, he just liked huge dicks. He didn't want them inside him. He just wanted to pretend they were his. To do this, he found it convenient and arousing to stick his cock in that man's ass. He worshipped the oversized male phallus. Stack was like the Holy Ghost. He was all-powerful and bigger than anyone else.

Stack stayed on the toilet, waiting for another expulsion of body fluids. He smiled at Guido. "You paid your ticket, kid. You can go."

"When can I see you again?" Guido wanted to be a parishioner of Stack's church and worship at his towering flesh altar often.

Stack shrugged.

Guido was no longer sure he was welcome, so he left. Stack breathed a sigh of relief. He preferred to fuck and forget.

❊ 6 ❊

HAPPY ENDING

Sheriff Whelan Dowd, aka "Stack," didn't know it, but he was lonesome and depressed. He didn't know because he had felt this way ever since he stopped being admired for his character and was only revered for the many inches of thick cock between his legs. Sex was terrific, but it didn't take away the loneliness. Preston had given him hope until he left without a proper goodbye. That broke his spirit. It only grew worse as he realized he didn't want to be with a woman, and he would need to seek out strangers from faraway towns to keep from being found out. It was indeed a tangled web woven from lies in the darkness of night.

Sitting in the station, bored and sweaty, Stack jumped when the phone rang. It was a call from Club Moderne, a fancy bar downtown. He didn't wait for details—a drunk needed to be hauled away.

At Club Moderne, Stack's heart broke. Babbling and carrying on was Lars Johnsson. A patron gave the sheriff a tip. "Apparently, his mother died last night."

Lars walked up to Stack and squeezed his left thigh. "Yep, it's real."

"Lars, what are you doing?"

"It's called a slip, Sheriff, and it feels fucking great!" Lars doubled over and vomited on the floor.

"Let's get you out of here."

Lars grew angry. "Why!?"

"You'll thank me in the morning."

In the cruiser, Lars bawled like a baby. Stack didn't interfere or try to quiet him down. As someone who never knew his mother, he had very little to say. Losing a father might be different.

"Stack, I'm all alone on this...in this world. Who's gonna love me now.?"

"It gets better." That was a white lie.

"I threw away everybody—my group of drunks. Whatcha I say to them? They's never let me back." His speech sounded more Swedish when he was drunk.

"Correct me if I'm wrong, Lars, but the only requirement for membership is the desire to quit drinking."

Lars leaned forward and fondly kissed Stack's neck. "I wouldn't join a club that would have me as a member."

"Groucho Marx."

Stack didn't want to throw Lars in jail with his mother still unburied. Against his better judgment, he brought Lars to the cottage.

"Where are we? Wait, don't tell me...is this the house of big dick?"

"It's my home, Lars."

"You're a legend, Stack. How many women do you fuck here each week?" Lars was at that drunk point where the filter shuts off. Stack didn't want to answer.

"None, am I right?" Lars was an obnoxious drunk.

"Yeah, you're right."

"Because I got the same problem, Stack. I can't fuck women. They get damaged."

"I never heard that."

"I kept my legend hidden from the world. You don't believe me?"

Lars undid his belt. Stack wanted to stop him, but

he was curious. Lars dropped his jeans, revealing a monster very much like Stack's. It was paler, with blonde pubic hairs, but it looked equal in length and breadth. Stack felt lightheaded. He understood now why people grew faint in the presence of his massive cock. Lars had the same problem.

"Lars, that's impressive. I think it's sleepy time." Stack patted the couch. Lars lay down on his side. His massive blonde cock spilled over sofa cushions and dangled to the floor.

"I'll get you a pillow and some blankets."

When he returned, Lars was no longer on the couch. He was half asleep in Stack's bed.

Stack sighed and took the couch.

In the morning, he awoke to the smell of coffee, sausages, and toast. Lars was in the kitchen cooking a greasy hangover breakfast. He smiled at the sheriff.

"This is an apology breakfast."

"Apology accepted."

They ate in silence. Lars blushed frequently.

Stack spoke first. "Lars, I'm sorry about your mother."

"They're cremating her today over in Butte." He stifled tears.

"She was a good woman."

"Did I ever meet your mom, Stack?"

"Don't know. I never met her myself."

Lars dipped his toast in the yolk. He stared at Stack.

"Look, I'm sorry for how I acted. I didn't mean to do that."

Stack smiled. "I'm not."

"Not what?"

"Not sorry you shared your secret with me. I wish mine were a secret."

Lars sipped his coffee. "So what now?"

"Do you need a ride to Butte?"

Stack helped Lars pick out a pleasant urn in his

price range. He drove the big blond fireman to his car at the Club Moderne.

"Are you going to be okay, Lars?"

"No, not really. I need company, and I got no one."

"I can come over and sit a spell." Stack had time. He was his own boss.

"You'd do that for me?"

"Sure I would. You're near 8th and Locust, right.?"

Lars needed a shoulder. He just needed to let out all the anguish and sadness that had built up while his mother fought to stay alive. Stack held him while he sobbed into his chest. Stack felt good having someone to hold who needed him. It was the exact wrong time to get a boner. But he did.

Lars couldn't see well through tears, but Stack's boner couldn't be missed. He frowned at the sheriff.

"Why are you hard?"

"Lars, I have no idea. It just feels so good holding you that I popped a boner."

Lars put a hand on Stack's cheek. He waited for the slap, but Lars came at him with his mouth. They tongue-kissed like a couple of teenagers. Stack wasn't the only one with a boner now. Lars rubbed his hand along Stack's left leg, feeling the long, thick meat trapped between his thigh and pant leg.

Stack shivered as though a goose walked over his grave. Lars was a high school crush. He felt guilty for turning his mourning into a makeout session.

"Lars, this isn't right, is it?"

"We're both orphans now. Who cares what we do?"

Stack shrugged. Good enough. He stood and peeled off his skin-tight polyester khakis, revealing a raging hard-on.

Lars ran his hands under Stack's shirt, massaging his belly and fingering his nipples. Stack was impressed with what he saw in the Swede's Levi's. He had seen Lars soft last night but hard, he was magnificent. Still playing with the sheriff's nipples, Lars Johnsson got to his feet and kissed Stack deeply.

Stack undid Johnsson's belt and let the pants pool around his ankle. Erect, the pale blond cock was like a log of uncut bologna. Lars grinned. They were evenly matched in length and thickness.

Lars teased, "We got two poppas; who's gonna play the mom?"

Stack didn't know why, but the size and power of the enormous cock hanging off of Lars made him want to submit. Lars invited Stack into his bedroom and stepped away.

In moments, Lars returned from the kitchen with a large tub of Crisco, a bowl of warm water, and a shampoo bottle. He cleaned the sheriff with a long, deep squirt from the bottle.

Stack emptied his bowels. It was clear.

Lars applied Crisco to the sheriff's opening, then greased up his arm. Stack panicked. He had no amyl nitrate, and no quaaludes. How would he get through it?

Lars warmed him up with a few fingers and then a full fist up Stack's astonished ass. The swede used his fist to find the opening at the end of the sheriff's rectum. Elbow deep, his hand reached up into Stack's left colon.

Stack expected far more pain. Lars did a lot of heavy lifting, and his forearm was thick and muscular. The Crisco was so slippery he couldn't fight the invasion. That must be why there was no pain. He couldn't push back. Having this handsome man's arm inside him felt better than quaaludes.

Lars liked dirty talk. He crooned into the sheriff's ear. "Oh yeah, sheriff, you like that arm in your cunt? Do you feel like a woman now? Where's your giant strong penis now, big man?"

To answer him, Stack swung hard and dick-slapped

Lars across the cheek. The look on the Swede's face was so comical he burst out laughing.

Lars didn't find it funny in the slightest. He slapped the sheriff hard with his free hand.

"You have no cock now. You are a woman. Hide that disgusting deformity."

Stack obeyed, tucking his cock under one leg. With Buck, he had felt dominated and wasn't sure he liked the submissive role. Lars was elbow-deep inside him, slapping him and humiliating him. It was much more potent. Stack could feel his leg rising with his stiffening cock. Lars had all the power now. Stack had to submit. He loved relinquishing control entirely to this man. Lars returned to his twisted, sweet nothings.

"You want me to tie you up? You want to be tied up like a pig? Little piggy wants rope?"

Stack nodded. In two shakes of a lamb's tail, his ass was empty, and both arms were bound to the bed knobs with greasy rope. He felt power draining out of him. Lars produced two small c-clamps.

"You know what these are for, little pig?"

The sheriff shook his head.

"These are for your titties. You like to have your titties pinched, yes?"

He nodded.

Lars rotated one clamp until it held his nipple firmly. He tightened the second one until Stack cried out in pain. Lars punched him to shut him up. Then he twisted the first one. The pain was blinding for a moment. Then his pupils closed down, and he felt a pleasant numbness everywhere in his body except for the two nipples. The burning stopped.

Lars said, "Now you are ready to accept my magnificent member into your vagina like the little slut whore you always wished you could be."

Stack was so turned on, his cock sprang free and

pointed skyward. Lars got more rope and tied his cock securely to his left leg.

"Are you ready for Lars to fuck your tight pussy?"

"Yes."

"Yes, what?"

"Yes, sir. Please, sir, fuck my pussy."

Stack hardly recognized himself. The arrogant, confident sheriff was begging a volunteer fireman to make a woman out of him with his baseball bat cock.

But it felt so good to let go. He didn't want control; he wanted to serve his new master. The years of stoic suffering in shame and silence vanished under the dominant command of the Swede.

"I will fuck you, and you will be my whore." Lars put his enormous cock head at the red, inflamed opening to Stack's ass. The sheriff whimpered.

"You will not cry. I forbid it. You will tell me how much you love my cock in you."

Stack nodded and grew quiet.

Lars pressed in. After a big arm, his cock was not as painful as he feared. But it hurt. He wanted to keep Lars happy, so he obeyed his orders. "Sir, your cock feels so good in my pussy."

Lars laughed. "I'm not even in you yet. This is the very tip. Do you want more?"

Stack nodded.

Lars rammed into the end of the rectum. He was cruel. Stack knew where to stop, but Lars wanted to inflict pain. He repeated the movement three or four times until Stack begged for mercy.

"Where else will I go, woman? Your cunt is too short."

"Go around the bend, please, sir?"

"The bend? Is there a bend in a vagina?"

"There is in mine, sir." To prove it, he twisted until Lars was pointed at the entryway.

Lars pushed forward, stretching Stack's inner ring to

the breaking point. He feared he would rip and lose blood. But Lars used a gentle rocking motion to work himself in deeper. Stack moaned.

"Is this crying? Are you a little bitch crybaby?"

"No, sir. Ooooh. Unh. It feels fucking great, sir."

Stack sucked air between his teeth.

"It sounds like you can't take me, whore. I thought you were a filthy slut."

"I am a filthy slut, sir. You are by far the biggest one to fuck my pussy. It doesn't hurt. You filled me with your cock."

Lars smiled. It was his first kind gesture since this crazy scene began. It made Stack want him more.

Lars had a solid back. He humped like a bull. Stack had never been this rough with Preston or anyone else. He wondered now why not. It was all pleasure and slippery cock moving hard at light speed in and out of his bottom. He had no control greased like he was. Lars had his legs pinned.

Lars slapped Stack's nipples and fiery darts of pain traveled to his groin, where they gurgled in his balls. His left knee was soaked with clear semen oozing from his rock-hard cock.

Lars began to breathe fast and shallow. He slapped Stack across the face. "I am going to plant babies in you now, woman. Do you want my baby seeds?"

Another nod.

"Say it!"

"Sir, I want you to come inside me and make me pregnant. I want to have your babies."

Lars wasn't expecting Stack to go off script, but it worked. His breaths changed again, and his powerful back muscles thrust his giant cock rapidly in and out of Stack's hole.

"My babies are coming. You're going to get pregnant!"

"Fuck me. Fill me up with your baby seeds. Make my cunt pregnant!"

Lars heard that and let loose with several months' worth of cum.

"Is your cunt wet?"

"Yes, sir. I feel so much semen in me; I think I'm gonna have triplets."

Lars pulled out roughly, leaving Stack empty inside. He wanted that massive cock in him again. Lars loosened the ropes on his leg, and Stack's gigantic cock swung skyward.

Lars looked at it in fascination.

"You were a good little slut, so I will reward you."

He reached inside Stack's ass and pulled out a glob of Crisco and semen. He put it into his own ass. He took a second helping and greased up the sheriff's pole.

"You are the man now. You may punish me."

Stack felt all the power handed back to him. His hands were still tied to the bed, but he could order Lars to untie them if he wanted to.

"Get these clamps off my tits, bitch."

Lars released them. They were sensitive and sore, but they felt sexy.

"Untie me, slut." Stack took on his angry lawman persona.

Lars obediently untied him. As soon as one hand was free, he backhanded Lars across the mouth, drawing a little blood.

"What have I done wrong, sir?"

"Shut the fuck up and sit on my cock, slut."

"You will rip my vagina wide open, sheriff."

"Tough shit. Now get your pussy on my cock and squat."

Lars had great difficulty getting the grapefruit head into his opening. Stack grabbed his hips and thrust upward into him. Lars screamed.

"How does the shoe feel on the other foot, bitch?"

"It hurts,"

"It hurts, what?"

"It hurts, sir."

Stack pulled his cock head out of Lars with a loud pop.

"Try again, whore."

Lars was able to take in the head this time. Once the corona was past his sphincter, the Swede could slide down the come-and-Crisco-slick pole until he reached the end of the rectum. His face was red. He was sweating like a whore in church. Stack wanted revenge. He pulled back an inch and then thrust upward hard five or six times. Lars bit his finger until it drew blood.

"Listen, whore, the last four inches of my dick are cold. You better figure out how to get my whole cock in your pathetic little pussy."

Lars exhaled and twisted, allowing the softball head to rip past his inner colon. He bounced a dozen times, stretching it enough to stop the pain, and then he sat down on Stack's lap.

"What a good little slut you are. I'm going to reward you with my cum."

He hefted Lars's perfect round buttocks and held him aloft. He fucked from below, his head slipping past the inner door in both directions. Lars dribbled clear semen onto the bed. Seeing his thick, elephantine cock and blond pubic hair got Stack excited. When the elephant's nose started to run, it was even better.

"You like that, bitch? I'm making your clitoris come."

Lars nodded. "Yes, sir, you're making me wet."

Stack rolled the fireman onto all fours and fucked him from behind. In the new position, where Stack's cock rubbed the prostate, the Swede's drooling penis was now nearly gushing with seminal fluid.

Stack let go of Lars and fucked him forward, so he landed face down on the bed. His penis was crushed, pointed backward in the V formed by his legs. It was just what Stack wanted. He lowered his hips until his balls dragged back and forth over Lars's cock head while he fucked him. Lars moaned.

"You like that? Do you like when I rub your clit with my big heavy balls?

"Yes, sir."

Lars grew hard from the rubbing. Stack got excited and fucked in a frenzy. His ass was still throbbing from the pounding Lars had just given him. Seeing his massive cock keeping Lars stretched open felt like justice.

"You ready, little whore? You want my cum up inside your uterus?"

"Get me pregnant, Sir. I want to get fat with your baby."

"My fat cock isn't enough? You need me to soak your cervix and make babies?"

"Please, sir. Yes, sir."

"Here you go, whore."

Stack fucked in a frenzy. He touched his sore nipples, and it shot straight to his balls. The signal traveled up his cock and out to his head. With that, he shot his load inside the Swede's ass.

"Fill my pussy. I need to be pregnant!" And Stack filled it. It was so full, it started squirting out the edges of the fireman's asshole. Stack collapsed on top of him, sweat from both men forming a slippery salve.

Stack stayed inside Lars for several minutes until his soft cock gushed out of him on a white sea of cum.

The two men dressed in silence. Now that their bizarre roles had ended, they were too embarrassed to look one another in the eye. Stack had no idea what had just happened. He was equally bewildered by how much he enjoyed it...and wanted to do it again.

Lars said, "If you want to do that again, I would like that very much."

Stack wanted to do all kinds of weird shit with Lars. But what if people found out?

"It's risky."

"You don't wish to be found out?"

"Of course not! They would either string us up or run us out of town."

"Who is 'they'? The sheriff?"

"Well, no, that's obvious."

"The town will organize a lynching party, perhaps?"

"It's not that, Lars. It's just…"

"You are afraid. Big lawman is afraid of being a faggot."

Stack backhanded Lars, who smiled.

"Stop it, you are turning me on!"

Stack glared at the Swede, and then both burst out laughing.

Lars pressed on. "You had nobody when Preston left."

"Who told you about Preston?"

"Nobody tells people when there is love. There is just love for all to see."

The sheriff burned with shame. "You mean everybody knew?"

"I don't think many people did because they could not imagine such a thing. I could, so I saw. Your lesbian friend Charlene saw."

"Charlene's a lesbian?"

"I knew about you in high school, Stack. You came to my track meets and saw only me. Nobody else was running, just me. And after I graduated, I came to your football games and saw only you."

"You did?"

"I have admired you for many years."

Stack had felt the same way.

"Why didn't you say anything?"

"I am allowed to be afraid too."

Stack suddenly felt like a kid. He had a lot to learn.

"Lars, I've been dying to ask this since earlier to-day...will you take out your dick and compare it with mine?"

"Sure, of course."

They stood side by side, their horse cocks dangling. In every way they were alike except color. Same thickness, same enormous head, hung down below the middle of the thigh.

"We're Dick twins. It's a strange curse, Lars."

"It can be a blessing when you find the right person. Like today."

The sheriff looked at Lars; they kissed. As their tongues intertwined, so too did their matching cocks, which grew hard and heavy at the same pace. Some holes were about to get stretched again.

AFTERWORD BY THE AUTHOR

The modern world despises differences. Most people seek comfort in sameness. Some people cannot seek sameness for any number of reasons. Perhaps they lost an arm in combat. Or maybe, like Cleve, they are two-spirit. Sheriff Dowd was different in several ways. He could not hide his huge appendage any more than a sailor could hide a missing arm. He was teased and ridiculed, yet no one felt sorry for him, for their jeers were covering over a deep insecurity. His cock dwarfed all others. All men felt small around Stack.

Stack was doubly burdened, for his early experiences with women created a complex. After Preston Twomey's initiation, he started a double life. This was a work of fiction, for every man he encountered wanted to have sex with him, even after seeing his grotesque penis. In truth, such a deformity frightens men. It draws them in with curiosity and fantasy, but once they realize the pain they would endure, it is all too much, and they leave. This is the curse of the extremely endowed.

Each encounter depicted is a situation where the Sheriff might have a chance in the real world. A young man with Amyl and quaaludes or an ex-army man who served many soldiers in the line of duty - both are potential mates. Some men have spent years inserting large objects in their anus - they, too, can handle a man like Whelan Dowd. Luckily, Stack was able to switch roles. This made it easy to find pleasure with a more rigid man like Guido Facchino.

The most preposterous fiction comes with the character of Lars Johnsson. He was teased in Sweden before getting to Anaconda, so he knew to hide his enormous shame from others by avoiding showers and public nudity. He is exactly like Sheriff Dowd, willing to take a man's or woman's role and equally endowed. This is a match made in Hollywood. In life, the men who bear the curse of abnormal size are seldom so lucky.

EDITOR'S NOTE

This afterword by Peter Schutes was a rare glimpse into the phallic psychology that drove his fantasies. We can only assume after reading it that the man was enormously endowed and suffered great loneliness because of it. Like the sheriff, his manhood was a legend that preceded him. His extraordinary size, rather than his extraordinary character, defined him among his social circle. We glimpse the bitterness that resulted.

Drugs don't appear in every novel, but they indeed take center stage in this one. Amyl Nitrate and Quaaludes were not illegal in the early 1960s, although both required a prescription. Some of Peter's books glorify modern drug use and condemn alcohol, a typical attitude in his early years as an author. He mentions Alcoholics Anonymous. That he knew about that program may mean he spent time in those rooms. We may never know, for that would violate one of the twelve traditions.

III

BUNKHOUSE BUDDIES

INTRODUCTION

It's no secret that many men became cowboys because they preferred the company and camaraderie of other rough-and-tumble men to the gentler life with women. These cowboys lived in groups of six to ten in bunkhouses - housing provided by the ranch owner at no cost or with reduced wages. The function of a traditional bunkhouse was to allow a young cowboy to find his footing and save money before he settled down and married. Not every cowboy had those particular plans. Many just wanted to be around other cowboys like themselves, confirmed bachelors. Buried deep in the Big Hole River Valley of Montana, the Cock Crow Ranch bunkhouse was entirely made up of lifelong bachelors. When a new cowboy came along, it was never certain if he would "fit in" with the bachelor lifestyle or if he would have to find a new ranch with morals more aligned with his own. A good fit was rare, but when that cowboy came along, he got to share in a brotherhood unlike any other. --Peter Schutes, 1961 Los Angeles, CA

BUCK

The sun had nearly set when the Trailways Bus stopped to let off a single passenger in front of Cock Crow Ranch. Mike eyed the new arrival from the top of the trail. He remembered his first night at the ranch so long ago and decided he would show the new kid some hospitality. He gently kicked Bandit in the side with his heels, and they cantered down the long trail to the highway.

Buck stepped down from the bus and thought the driver had made a mistake. The fence ran uninterrupted for as far as the eye could see. This couldn't be the entrance to a ranch. He turned to question the driver but only tasted dust as the bus pulled away from the shoulder. Buck would need to convert his duffel into a backpack for the endless walk to his new home.

Cursing under his breath, he threw down the bag and sat on it. He put his head in his hands and waited for frustration to survive. Working when angry only leads to mistakes and regrets.

Speaking of regrets, he wished he had worn a more recent pair of jeans. These Wranglers were two years old, and although soft and worn, they were too tight through the crotch, ass, and thighs, all three of which had grown considerably since he had bought them. The new pair of Lee's was stiff, but it was a more generous cut and accommodated all of Buck's bulging parts. He almost missed the tiny speck on the horizon that grew as it approached. Soon he could make out a horse and rider. Buck breathed a sigh of relief and stood.

The new kid was wrestling with his duffel bag when Mike rode up on Bandit.

"You look like you could use a little help," Mike offered.

"Gosh, sir, that would be awfully nice."

"Name's Mike, and you are...."

"Buck." He offered his hand, and they shook. Mike noticed immediately how soft the skin was on Buck's palms. It clashed with Mike's rough, calloused, rope-burned paws.

"Buck, I'm guessing you answered that ad in the paper. Did Dick offer you a bunk?"

"Yeah, Dick Burns wrote me back and said the bed was mine if I wanted it."

Mike had been busy focusing on strapping Buck's bag to his horse, so he was surprised when he looked up. Buck was just staring at Mike with big watery blue eyes. Blond curly locks of hair framed his head. Mike made an involuntary groan. This kid was too pretty and soft to last long on the Cock Crow Ranch. He sized the boy up. Buck was built wide. It was impossible to tell if he was muscle or fat under his fleece denim jacket. That would make all the difference. Muscle, he stays; fat, he goes. Mike had nothing against fat boys; he was just acutely aware that they weren't cut out for the job Buck was taking.

With luggage secured, Mike mounted Bandit and pointed to the stirrup. "Left boot in there."

Before Mike could so much as offer Buck a hand up, he was already up and seated behind him. Well, he certainly knew horses. That was a plus.

"What did you do before this, Buck?"

"I was in the Army for a little while, but it didn't work out too well."

Mike could feel the awkward pause as Buck evaded further discussion of his military career. "How is it you know how to mount a horse"?

"I lived on a farm in Tennessee. We had a few horses. Used to ride every day."

This kid was more interesting than he first appeared.

"You ever lived in a bunkhouse before"?

"Well, yeah, a barracks in the military. Not ever on a cattle ranch."

"I gotta warn you, the guys in there aren't all as nice as me." Mike grinned.

"Am I gonna have to beat the biggest one in a fight or something"? Buck didn't sound scared.

"I doubt it. This ain't jail...feels like it sometimes."

Buck leaned in and asked, "They got any pretty girls around here"?

Bandit came to an abrupt halt in front of the bunkhouse. It was an old, squat building perched on a makeshift porch of concrete and stone. The look was classic Great Plains with unpainted wood, ancient double-hung windows, and a shingle roof. It had been a sod house in a former life. Now it was just slave's quarters for the ranch hands.

Buck dismounted gracefully and unconsciously offered a hand to Mike, who swatted it away. Buck blushed.

"Sorry, it's an old habit."

"It was sweet, kid. I get it."

Buck winked conspiratorially, "Now, about my earlier question...about girls."

Mike guffawed. "About 20 miles down the Big Hole River is the closest town. They got a few bars. The girls you meet ain't exactly the kind you wanna bring home."

Buck nudged Mike.

"Are you saying you brung one home?"

"Hell no!" Mike blushed and objected vehemently.

The look that passed across Buck's face was one Mike knew well. It was recognition, the bond of bachelorhood. Mike decided to go for it.

"Handsome guy like you, ain't you got a girl already?"

Now it was Buck's turn to blush.

"Thought not." Mike winked as he unhitched the duffel and handed it to the newbie.

Buck smiled with mischief. "Thanks."

"Let me introduce you to the men." Mike opened the weather-beaten door and gestured for Buck to enter.

MIKE

Inside the bunkhouse was mayhem. Four ranch hands in various states of undress were fighting for their place under one of the two shower heads. Towels snapped bare asses, red welts rising to howls of protest and pain. When Mike and Buck entered, the horseplay came to a gradual stop.

An olive-skinned man with a handlebar mustache and a sunken chest gave a gleaming white grin.

"This the new guy, Mike"? He stepped forward from the pack of buckaroos, revealing his naked body. Buck swallowed hard and tried not to blush.

"I'm Sal. I cook your supper." He extended his hand, which Buck took firmly and shook with masculine vigor. Buck tried to focus on Sal's face, but his eyes kept drifting downward. He had seen some big ones in the army, but Sal's short stature and skinny legs made for a very impressive frame to a whopper cock.

Of course, Sal was used to the attention he got from men. No man in his right mind could look away from such an impressive package.

"I'm Italian. That's where I get it from."

"Get what"? Buck tried to feign innocence. He was greeted by guffaws from the whole crew.

Mike stepped in. "Easy, guys. Don't scare away the

new arrival." He turned to Buck, "Sal is hung huge. We all check it out. That's what men do."

Buck regained his composure and blurted, "Huge. No shit. I pity the girl who marries you."

Sal didn't take offense. "I don't think I'm the marrying kind, Buck." He finished it off with a wink.

A stocky, dark-haired cowboy wrapped in a towel stepped forward and offered his hand. "I'm D. I ride drag."

Buck took his firm hand and shook. "Drag, so you ride behind the herd, right?" Buck knew a little about cattle—enough to sound like he knew more.

"Yep, I come from behind and head up the rear." D grinned lasciviously. "You're gonna be my replacement. Going to Louisiana to work on a rig. Leave next week."

"So you training me?"

D nodded and took a pinch of Copenhagen from a tin before tucking it back at the waist of his towel.

Buck heard a voice in his ear and whirled around.

"Name's Will Dewey." An extremely attractive older gentleman with pale green eyes and a gray beard stepped forward and offered his hand. "I'm the flanker."

"Pleased to meet you, sir." Buck liked the look and feel of older men. He felt protected with Will. Will still wore his dirty jeans and a moth-eaten pearl snap shirt. Buck wondered what Will Dewey, the flanker, looked like when he was out of his clothes. He would find out soon enough.

The last guy to come lumbering forward was a towering furry beast of a man. "Aloysius, but everyone calls me Bear." Buck felt his hand disappear into his giant paw. "I ride swing." Buck took in this man's furry body. Hidden beneath the fur were gigantic muscles. Pectoral muscles the size of two dinner plates connected to cantaloupe-sized shoulders flanking a sinewy neck as thick as a small tree trunk. His waist was too wide to support a towel, so he was forced to hold it in place between his meaty fingers. Buck could just make out the outline of a semi-hard cock in the same league as Sal's, although it appeared smaller against such a big frame.

So these were the new bunk mates that Buck would be with nearly 24 hours a day. Sal, the cook with the dick of death; D, the drag who comes from behind; Will Dewey, the handsome older flanker with a fatherly demeanor; and Bear, the furry swing with swing to spare. Then there was Mike.

"So, Mike, I guess you ride point," Buck correctly surmised.

"Yep, I'm always at the front. I get the first plate of Sal's supper and take the first shower when the water's still hot."

Buck smiled, "So you're top dog."

"If I tell you to do something, you will damn well do it!" Mike's tone took a sinister turn.

"Y-yes, sir," Buck said.

The darkness lifted, and Mike gave a friendly smile. "Attaboy." He then turned on the crew and snarled. "Which one of you cocksuckers took a shower before me?" Despite being outnumbered 4 to 1, Mike's commanding tone turned the bunkmates into a subservient, apologetic pile of excuses.

"We figgered you was out gettin' the new guy, so the water would still be hot by the time you got back."

"You better fuckin' hope you figgered right!" Mike kicked off his boots, pulled his shirt over his head, and undid his jeans. When he bent over to pull them off, Buck got a glorious view of the two white mounds that formed his thick ass. As Mike lifted each leg and stepped out, Buck even got a view of his puckered hole and his big dangling balls between his meaty thighs. The tip of his soft dick winked in and out of sight from behind the generous balls.

Fully nude, Mike stormed into the bathroom and

turned on the water. A cloud of steam formed, and the whole room breathed a sigh of relief.

"Buck!" Mike called angrily as if Buck had broken a plate or pissed on the neighbor's roses. "Get your ass in here!"

Buck headed towards the bathroom, but Bear held out an arm to stop him. "Get naked," he said softly.

Buck yanked off his boots. He wasn't sure where to put them until Will pointed to the empty bunk.

Mike was twice as cross when he yelled, "Buck, what the fuck is taking so long?"

"Hang on, almost naked!" He shucked his clothes as quickly as he could. When he looked up, he saw all four men looking hungrily at him as if he were a hearty beef stew. Buck was too stressed to care.

He skidded into the shower, sliding on a bar of soap, nearly colliding with Mike.

Mike pushed Buck against the shower wall and held him by his shoulders. The two men sized each other up. Mike had a light brown coating of chest hair that circled his silver dollar-sized nipples. A treasure trail led to a well-trimmed bush of pubic hair perched atop his dick. Mike had an average-sized uncut dick hanging soft, but it grew longer without stopping as he took in Buck's beauty. By the time it stood straight out from his hips, it was thin but well above average length, his foreskin nearly invisible stretched along its length. His balls hung low, two plums in a tan leather bag.

Buck had only blond peach fuzz in a few places. His chest was smooth and sculpted. He resembled a Greek statue because of his curly locks of hair and his elegant hips, buttocks, and legs. A tangled bush of wiry blond pubic hair graced his plump manhood. Seeing Mike grow hard caused Buck to swell. His tiny balls only helped make his thick meat look even thicker.

Mike leaned forward, his cock brushing Buck's belly, and whispered, "I need the soap. Can you reach it?"

Buck nodded. He squatted down, slipping the soap out from under his foot. He was at eye level with Mike's long, narrow cock. Mike swung his hips and smacked Buck on the cheek. It was playful but demanding. Buck looked up at Mike and handed him the soap. Mike laughed and dropped it again.

"Not so fast, buckaroo. You got work to do."

Mike poked Buck repeatedly on the lips until he opened his mouth to let his insistent member enter. Mike wasted no time. He held Buck by the ears and jammed his overlong narrow cock into the back of Buck's mouth. Buck gagged and tried to pull away, but Mike shook his head.

"No, boy. You know how to do this. You got them cocksucking lips. I bet they kept you real busy in the army."

Buck retched again, then focused on suppressing his gag reflex. Mike was right. Buck sucked so many cocks in the army that he lost count. He was an expert, but even experts need a little time to prepare to accommodate a dick as long as Mike's. A few more waves of nausea washed over him, each less powerful than the previous. Meanwhile, Mike insistently banged at his tonsils, only getting two-thirds of his length sucked.

"What you waiting for, boy? Jerk the rest." Mike had no idea what was about to happen.

Buck smiled inwardly as he relaxed his throat muscles and let Mike's long cock slide its entire length down his throat. Mike gasped in astonishment as his balls smacked into Buck's chin. Buck knew right away that he was the first to give Mike the full treatment.

Mike couldn't believe it. As far as he knew, he was too big. He didn't know there was anywhere else his cock could go. Buck blew his mind and body. The feeling of his cockhead being squeezed by the pharyngeal muscles and his frenulum being tickled by the epiglottis caused his knees to quiver. He momentarily lost balance, but Buck held Mike's hips and pressed them against the shower wall to steady him.

This sudden contact between the two men pushed Mike past the limit. He was going to blow. Buck tasted pre-ejaculate and knew it was almost time. Mike forcedly grabbed his blond curly hair, holding his face against his crotch, allowing him to thrust even deeper into the newly discovered paradise at the back of Buck's throat.

Mike began emitting a soft moan. Buck knew that making a similar sound should increase Mike's pleasure. He whimpered in anticipation. He looked up to catch Mike's eye.

Mike looked down at the cherub who so masterfully brought him to the verge of climax. Their eyes locked; it was too intense. Mike closed his eyes and softly whispered, "Oh fuck, Oh fuck. I'm gonna come. I'm gonna come." He pounded furiously into Buck's throat, feeling a surge of energy forming deep in his ball sack. The energy became heat, and the heat began its journey up the length of Mike's shaft. It gathered speed and melted into a flaming hot river of come, which erupted in bolt after ropy bolt down Buck's throat, then filled his mouth. A few last cobwebs of semen splattered on the boy's face.

Buck reached for the soap to hand it to Mike as if nothing had happened. Mike soaped his cock and balls, then turned and soaped his asscrack. Buck tried to stand up, but Mike pushed him down gently.

"Oh no, you don't. Now it's your turn."

Mike presented his ass to Buck and spread the cheeks, revealing his hole. Buck didn't ask questions; he buried his face in Mike's crack and greedily licked his butthole.

Mike moaned softly. "Deeper, man, go deep."

Buck obeyed, extending his tongue as far as it would go up Mike's ass. Mike wiggled his hips in a rather feminine manner, which surprised Buck but didn't slow him down. Mike chattered away while Buck tongued him. "Ooh yeah. Oh, you like that pussy? You gonna make me a little girl? You wanna fuck my tight little pussy"?

Buck rolled his eyes and thought, "It takes all kinds." He had to admit the power reversal was making him horny. Big point man, top dog, asking the new guy to fuck him and make him a girl. Buck felt himself get harder. He had a few days worth of cum built up, and he wanted to release it badly. He stood up and rubbed his hard cock up and down the crack of Mike's ass.

Mike spit three times into his hand and rubbed his asshole, then Buck's dick, until they were both slick with spit. Mike guided Buck to the entrance. Buck was tempted to return the favor and jam his dick in without mercy, but he knew that a dick as thick as his could do damage if not handled properly. He put the head in and pushed until he felt resistance, then backed up a quarter of an inch to give things time to adjust.

Mike was a whiny bitch all of a sudden. "Come on, man, what are you waiting for? Fuck my pussy! Make me your bitch."

Buck sighed inwardly. Mike could not possibly be ready yet. But then he started pushing back, impaling himself on the first 3 inches of Buck's dick. Buck had a football-shaped cock. He knew its dimensions well. Everything was within the range of normal the first three inches, four inches in, and he was as big around as a wine bottle.

Mike was insistent. "Put it in, please"!

Buck figured he wouldn't often have this opportunity to ravage a man with impunity. He dreaded the blood and likely early end to the fun, but it would feel good giving Mike the most painful minute of his life.

He held Mike by the hips and, with one swift movement, thrust to the hilt.

Mike moaned softly. Buck pulled back, stretching

Mike like a rubber band, then jammed his cock in all the way again. He pulled back a third time to check for blood, but his dick was squeaky clean.

"Mike, how are you able to take this."?

"I live with Sal and Bear. Now fuck me like you mean it, punk"!

Hearing this gave Buck renewed drive. He was salty as fuck and needed to get off badly. He started banging Mike with the same vigor he had taken a few minutes earlier down his throat. It was a revenge fuck, but it was more than that. He could see Mike's face, overcome with desire and pleasure. Each time Buck brought his cock halfway out, Mike hummed with pleasure, feeling his sphincter stretch and shrink over and over. Buck reached around to play with Mike's nipples. He hadn't noticed, but they were long and thick, like fleshy thimbles. With each squeeze and twist, Mike cried out in ecstasy. He was making a lot of noise.

Mike wanted Buck all the way inside him. He lifted one leg, and Buck held it aloft, making the path from his cock to Mike's hole as short as possible. This allowed Buck to penetrate Mike fully, stretching him deep inside. To Buck, this felt like a fleshy glove stroking his manhood.

Buck was used to being the cocksucker. He had rarely been with a man or a woman this way, at least not for long. They always cried out in pain and begged him to stop, ending in a hand job and regret. Hearing Mike grunt, "Don't Stop! Fuck me harder!" was unprecedented. It turned Buck into a fucking machine. His hips pounded against Mike's backside, each thrust becoming more violent than the last. He unleashed years of pent-up rage and frustration, and Mike absorbed it like a sponge.

Fucking is supposed to be like this. Each person gets pleasure by giving pleasure to the other. This was Buck's first proper fuck, where he could pound and stretch with wild abandon. A wave of pleasure washed over him, and he saw it transfer to Mike, who shivered with delight.

Another wave came and transferred to Mike. It was a rhythm building between the two of them. Mike looked back at Buck, sweat pouring down his face. His pupils were pinpricks. He silently mouthed some nasty talk to himself, lost not only in his own bubble of ecstasy but feeding off of and giving back to Buck's pleasure. The wave came again, and Mike's eyes rolled back into his head. The waves were coming at closer intervals now. This was nothing like the buildup to come from jacking off. This was a bioenergetic circuit, increasing in amplitude with each passing spark.

Buck needed to satisfy a curiosity. For a moment, he pulled completely out. He saw what he had hoped: Mike's ass was so stretched that it stayed gaping open.

Mike turned and hissed. "Stop lookin' and fuck my pussy, tenderfoot."

Buck reinserted himself and found that the waves were far apart again. But he kept picturing Mike gaping wide open, which sped things up. Mike was pushing to meet his every thrust. He played with his own long skinny cock, which had recovered from its earlier explosion and now stood up rock-hard past his belly to his chest. He played with himself gently at first, then more vigorously as the rhythm of the fuck got more intense.

Seeing Mike jerk his long cock, and picturing the gaping hole in his mind's eye was the magic combination. Urgent spasms replaced the waves.

Mike increased his stroking in response, and in moments, Buck was in the home stretch.

Mike whimpered. "Oh yeah. Oh, baby." His masculinity was cast aside to allow him to be a receptacle for Buck; it was all a turn-on now.

"You want me to fuck that pussy?" Buck hollered.

Mike cried out, "Yes!"

"You want me to shoot my load in your girly little pussy?"

"Make me pregnant! Make a baby in me!"

Buck didn't care how ridiculous that sounded; he just knew that he wanted to spew come up this man's cunt.

"Are you ready?"

"Do it! Fill me with all your seed!"

"Take it, bitch!"

And with those words, Buck let loose a torrential flood of cum inside Mike's gaping ass. Mike was so wrapped up in his baby-making fantasy he scarcely noticed that he had shot a load of his own all over his face, neck, and chest.

Buck was so turned on he just kept pumping out more and more come. He could feel his cock growing slick with it as he slowly thrust back and forth.

They stood belly to back, locked at the waist, until Buck finally squeezed out the last vestiges of come. He pulled his slowly deflating prick out of Mike's cavernous ass and felt it slap hard against his thigh.

He watched in morbid fascination as Mike began to eject cum from his ass into his hand. His hand was full when he brought it to his lips and drank the semen like water from a warm spring. He returned his hand, and it filled again. Mike offered it to Buck, who politely declined. Astonishingly, the cum kept dripping out of him, and he kept drinking; Buck thought he must have spilled an impossible amount.

Mike turned around to him and whispered, "It's not just yours."

With that, he turned the shower back on, cleaned his hole and cock, then soaped up Buck for good measure.

When they left the bathroom, they were greeted with silent stares. Buck wanted to die of embarrassment. The men were whispering between themselves and nodding, but Buck couldn't hear what they were saying. Mike presented Buck like a show pony. "Gentleman, the meat has passed inspection. He is yours to sample as you please." Buck looked around the room at the hungry eyes eating him alive. He grinned. This was going to be a good year.

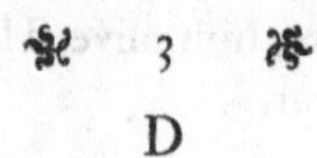

D

Sunrise was hours away when Buck was shaken awake by D, the drag, who would train him to lead from behind.

"Sal started breakfast. I wouldn't want you to miss it; it's a long hard day ahead."

Indeed, Buck could smell bacon. He yanked up his jeans and threw on a t-shirt, stepping into his boots. In less than a minute, he was seated at the end of the table next to Mike. Sal served plates of eggs, grits, and bacon with biscuits and gravy. Plates arrived in order of seniority, so Mike started in first, and Buck was last.

Mike ate slowly, waiting for Buck to get his helping. He knew this kid was too good to keep all for himself, but he still felt the urge to claim his property. The kid wasn't the biggest, but he was definitely the thickest guy Mike had ever taken. He felt a hint of shame about getting plowed and making baby talk, and he didn't like it. To avoid his feelings, he smacked Buck on the side of his head and bellowed, "Slow down!" as Buck had since gotten his helping and was wolfing it down with gusto.

Buck looked up with gravy in the corner of his mouth, startled. "Yes sir, sorry sir."

He was a quick study in obedience, which made Mike want him all the more. The others around the table did their best to pretend nothing was happening. They knew that as long as Mike stayed focused on Buck, they could avoid his abuse.

Buck wiped the gravy from his mouth with his finger and sucked it clean. He knew how to distract men like Mike. Buck batted his long eyelashes and held his head hangdog, waiting for his next order. The only sound was the clanking of stainless steel cutlery against aluminum plates and hungry cowhands breathing through their noses. Buck saw Mike break. One second he was on the verge of giving the boy a savage beating; the next, he had released the boy from his control for the world to have at him. Mike no longer owned him.

The men around the table all sensed this power struggle but knew better than to pounce on Buck while Mike was still smarting from the battle. There would be plenty of time today to find themselves alone with the new boy. They weren't exactly sure what happened in the shower last night, but Mike had never looked so satisfied. They all wondered what Buck had up his sleeve...or down his pant leg that got Mike in such a twist.

Buck rode with D behind the herd until they reached the open grazing land along the Big Hole River. Once the cattle were munching happily on the long prairie grass, D took a tobacco break in the shade of a scrub oak. He offered a pinch to Buck, who politely declined.

D took time to critique Buck's technique and offered to teach him roping skills. "You're the last line of defense. If any calf gets funny ideas and tries to run in the opposite direction, it's gonna be you who's gotta rope him and send him back to the herd."

Buck nodded. "You could definitely help me out if you teach me to lasso. I mean, we all did it in FFA, but that was a few years ago."

D smiled. "You're in luck. There ain't no better roper in Montana."

They started with the basics. Buck got the loop spinning, then moved it overhead, to the side, and finally tossed it over a tree stump. D was pleased, but he could see the kid was still green. It was time to take it up a notch.

"Okay, kid, I'm gonna run past you, and you gotta try and get me by the legs."

"Like tackle you"?

"No, dipshit, with the rope!" But then he saw Buck's mischievous smile and knew it was not a serious question.

D favored the color black. Head to toe, from his hat to his boots, he was the man in black. It would make it tricky to get the rope under his feet. D ran past him a half dozen times before Buck finally snagged him and took him down. He ran to D and wrapped his wrists tightly, just like he would do to a calf's front legs. Then he bound his feet to his wrists.

"Okay, that was good." D chuckled, waiting for Buck to release him. Buck stood surveying his handy work, hands on his hips. Buck licked his lips and thought about his prize. D struggled to get loose, but Buck had tied a perfect half-hitch. He was stuck.

Buck looked D up and down. "You wear more black than Johnny Cash." Is your underwear black too?

D struggled to upright himself like a cockroach on its back. "Why don't you untie me, and I can show you."

Buck shook his head. "I'm gonna find out myself." He bent down and undid the top button of D's black jeans. D wriggled in protest. Buck went for another button and revealed D's pubes.

"Is that what you wanted to show me?" At the third button, the top of D's shaft was exposed.

D quit struggling and gave in. The kid took the

rope's end and tossed it over a low oak branch. He tugged hard, and D was hoisted in the air. Buck tied him off like a rack of meat swinging in the air. He loosened D's belt so his jeans would easily slide down to his ankles, leaving him naked and erect. D was enjoying Buck's domination, despite himself.

D usually kept to himself. He avoided the horseplay and sex with the other men. It conflicted with his upbringing in a proper Christian household. He knew what went on out here was sinful, if not enjoyable. He avoided sex but didn't skip it entirely. Mike made sure he got passed around once or twice a month. At first, D screamed from the pain. After a week with Bear going at him nonstop, he moved past the pain and discomfort and entered a painless sinful bliss. He learned how a man's ass can give and receive pleasure. He'd never been hogtied before.

D looked at Buck and wondered if he could be any more painful than Bear. He saw Buck rubbing his crotch and traced the outline. His cock was nowhere near as long as Sal or Bear, but it was shaped differently.

Buck was a gentleman. He used his tongue to lube up D's ass with generous gobs of spit. He walked around to D's head and rubbed his crotch in his face. D felt something different about Buck underneath those Wranglers. His dick was just average length, but the middle part was thicker than his wrist. To demonstrate, Buck pulled his jeans down slowly, letting the football flop out and stand at half-mast, straining under the weight of its midsection. He put the tip into D's mouth.

"D, you're gonna want to get as much spit on there as you can, okay."

Mouth full, D nodded and stretched his jaws apart. He struggled with the thick middle and wasn't able to lube it up well.

"I'm gonna be generous with you," Buck pulled his

dick out and spit in his hand, stroking his slippery saliva up and down the length of his shaft. He took one of D's black socks and shoved it in his mouth. Inwardly, he felt sorry for D, who probably wouldn't enjoy this forced sex. But D's cock was rock hard, and even dribbled a little. Buck frowned and asked, "Do you want this, you little slut"?

D nodded in the affirmative.

"You want this cock in your ass"?

D nodded even more vigorously.

"Do you want me to untie you"? D shook his head no. Perfect. Buck had captured his prize; he played the game and won. Now it was time for a reward.

Buck stuck a finger in D to test the waters. It was a tight hole, but his finger went in quite easily. He took it out and sniffed it. He smiled.

"You cleaned real good, didn't you"? D nodded.

Buck popped his small head past D's sphincter and pushed forward until he met resistance. D's truss moved slightly forward, emphasizing that Buck was at the limit of D's resilience. D sucked in air between his teeth. Buck pushed D's buttocks away from him, providing momentary relief. Gently, Buck let go and let D slide back down further on his cock. D winced but kept silent, breathing through his nostrils.

Buck pushed D away again, and this time he dropped a big ball of spit right at the widest part of his cock. Buck let go suddenly, and D was taken by surprise as he slid back down onto Buck's cock with enough force to pass the widest part, which was slick with spit.

D saw stars as the pain hit him like a brick. He thrashed and kicked, screaming "Mother of Christ!" through the dirty sock. And then the pain was gone. Buck was balls deep, where the base of his cock grew narrow. D breathed a sigh of relief until Buck pushed him away, forcing him to take the widest part in reverse.

White hot heat burned in his ass, but it was less than the first time.

Again D felt relief as Buck pushed him further away from that painful wide spot. Buck let go; D swung like a pendulum right past the impasse and once more impaled himself fully on Buck's cruel cock.

D thought about those painful nights with Bear. He was thick and much longer than Buck, but he didn't have Buck's unforgiving wide spot that caused him to thrash in pain and ecstasy each time he passed it. Mike was long and skinny - the perfect shape for fucking ass. Buck was obscenely thick in the middle, but each thrust brought a fraction less pain and more of that good tingle you get with ass-fucking.

By now, Buck had built up a rhythm. He was using gravity to his advantage, pushing D away and letting him collide ass to hips, over and over. D was still wincing with pain, but each thrust caused so much pleasure; Buck couldn't care less what his hogtied hostage felt at this point. Buck only felt the tight, smooth circumference of D's hole, stretching wide and snapping closed as it passed back and forth over Buck's widest part.

D fell into the zone where the pain of having his ass ravaged, combined with the extreme discomfort of being hogtied and the humiliation of being gagged with his own sock, created a hybrid sensation that was neither pain nor discomfort. It was something else entirely; a sublime pleasure made up of physical and psychological sensations in concert. He felt helpless, vulnerable, and aroused. Being used so thoroughly gave him a sense of purpose. He wanted to give the kid pleasure. He looked down at his soft cock, leaking a clear fluid. More kept coming with each stretching pass. He had heard of this but had never felt it before. Buck was giving him an anal orgasm. With his hands and feet bound and his anal cavity filled with another man's invading flesh, he grew intoxicated.

Buck noticed D's drooling dick and felt a flush of pride. He was fucking him so well that it made him come hands-free, even soft. The fluid formed a puddle at the edge of D's waist, then dripped in long thin threads onto the dirt below.

A familiar warmth began to build in Buck's loins. He pulled out completely, then pounded his swollen member back through D's gaping hole until his hips crashed into D's buttocks, sending him swinging back, exposing Buck's full manhood, and a pendulum cycle formed.

D was past the point of pain, so deep in pleasure that he couldn't think of a word to describe the feeling. Ecstasy? Maybe. The pressure of Buck's cock was causing his cock to leak faster and faster. Buck threw his head back and muttered, "Aw fuck. Aw shit. I'm close, man, so fucking close." In a brief gesture of kindness, D's captor reached out and yanked the sock from his mouth.

"You like that?" he asked, "You like being tied up like an animal?"

D whispered, "Yes. Yes, sir."

"Get ready for it. I'm, I'm...ohhh!" Buck sprayed the walls of D's ass with his thick, hot cum.

D felt wet inside and out. He was drenched in sweat and his own leaky seminal fluid, and now he had Buck's thick white gravy deep in his rectum.

At that moment, Buck locked eyes with the helpless handsome cowboy. He had dark brown hair, almost black, and a thin mustache framing his full lips. Buck had never wanted this before, but he had a prisoner, so he did it - he planted his lips on D's.

D was startled, taken aback, then suddenly very, very aroused. He leaned into Buck's kiss, letting his lips part. Their tongues touched and retreated. Then they touched again, only Buck was more forceful this time, and D was more receptive. He let Buck into his mouth, and they kissed like a couple of horny teenagers at Inspiration Point.

The intimacy of the kiss caused D's cock to stiffen. Buck felt it throbbing insistently at his belly. Without asking, Buck knelt and took D's boner into his mouth and sucked him off. D had already had one type of orgasm, and two seemed greedy. But he wasn't in charge. His attempts to bring Buck back to his mouth for more kissing were met with swats of annoyance. D's ass was wet with cum. Buck easily slid a finger up to the knuckle. A river of cum rushed past the digit, cascading in rivulets to the mossy ground below.

D didn't take long. Buck's finger found the perfect spot. D felt every drop of Buck's come draining from his loose, open hole. His wrists and ankles burned, and his shoulders ached. He could see Buck's still hard cock standing at attention. He marveled at the shape and size. He could scarcely believe that it had just been inside him. And that sent him over the edge.

He bucked rhythmically, pumping a thick load into Buck's mouth. Buck didn't spit, and he didn't swallow. He stood, plunged his still-hard cock back up D's chute, then leaned forward and locked lips. D parted his lips and let his own come into his mouth. Buck shared it with him like a man milkshake.

Buck stayed inside D until he grew soft. Nature took over, and peristalsis forced Buck out of D's sore, stretched hole.

When Buck cut him loose, it Took D a full five minutes to regain his balance. Leaning on Buck, D limped with him back to the horses. Time had passed quickly.

Buck remarked, "We were fuckin' till the cows come home."

And indeed, they had. They rejoined the crew just in time to ride drag back to the bunkhouse.

❊ 4 ❊

SAL

Sal had a generous supper waiting for the men
when they returned. There was still a lot of work
to do before sundown, so they had to eat quickly.
Mike looked at D and asked, "Did you show Buck the
ropes?"

D and Buck exchanged a private look. Buck answered, "He sure did!"

Mike roared, "I didn't ask you, little bitch; I asked
D." In any normal household, this would be followed by
a stunned silence. But here in the bunkhouse, the men
just kept right on eating. Mike's bark was worse than
his bite.

"Yeah, Mike. I'd say this boy can lasso and hogtie a
steer as good as any of us now."

Mike pointed to D's wrists. "What happened
there"?

Without missing a beat, D said, "Rope burn. One
feisty calf nearly dragged me into the river."

The guys nodded, as this had happened before to all
of them. Buck wondered what D would say if they
could see his ankles. D was gonna shower in his socks
tonight, no doubt.

When the plates were cleared, Sal asked Mike if he
could borrow Buck to help with the dishes. Mike

grunted his approval, and the men cleared out, leaving Sal and Buck alone at the sink.

To pass the time, Sal started asking Buck the usual litany of small talk questions:

Where are you from?

Where are your parents?

You got a girl back home?

Buck hated small talk.

"Sal, that's short for Salvatore, right"?

Sal smiled. "Nope. My name's Giovanni."

"So why Sal."

"Short for Salami."

They both chuckled.

Buck decided to turn it up a notch.

"Sal, what keeps you here in a bunkhouse full of men?"

"Well, Buck, like most of us here, I prefer the company of men."

This was going right where he hoped it would.

"So how do you keep that huge cock of yours satisfied"?

Sal didn't blush, didn't drop a plate,

"Mostly, I gotta take care of it myself."

"Let me see it again. I didn't get a very good look last time."

Sal sighed and dropped his pants, revealing a soft thick cock hanging nearly down to his knees. Buck caught his breath, then whistled.

"Damn! You got one huge cock, Sal."

Sal seemed bored. "I'm only 5'2". It's not as big as it looks."

Buck pressed forward. "It looks so heavy. Can I hold it?"

Sal shrugged sadly. "Sure, why not?" You could never take it. Not a greenhorn like you,"

"You don't know that. Shit!" Buck exclaimed as he lifted Sal's Leviathan cock and felt its heft and weight."

"Kid, trust me. You could never take me."

"You wanna bet?" Buck looked hungrily at Sal's endowment.

There was a weariness to Sal's voice that told a sad, familiar tale...eager men and women ready to take on the monster until it hurts them. Then they run screaming bloody murder. Buck knew a little of this weariness himself. But Buck wasn't a coward.

"Hey, let's me and you go sit on my bunk, and I'll show you a couple of magic tricks."

Sal frowned, but his curiosity was piqued. "You gonna make my dick disappear?"

"Yeah, actually. See, I got a couple of talents you might like to learn about."

Sal kicked off his boots and shucked his jeans. He walked straight to Buck's bunk and sat defiantly, arms crossed, skeptical.

Buck knelt before him and lifted Sal's flaccid cock to his lips and kissed it. "This poor baby needs some lovin'."

Buck put the tip in his mouth and licked it like a lollipop.

Sal protested, "Kid, you can't possibly fit that in your mouth. It may fit now, but not for long."

Buck took the flesh lollipop out of his mouth and said, "My family's part snake. Watch." Buck unhinged his lower jaw and put his whole fist in his mouth. Sal was impressed.

"How did you do that?"

"Sssssss!" Buck joked. "Now shut up and let me suck your cock!"

Buck folded Sal's soft cock into his mouth and began applying suction. Sal leaned back and smiled. "Here it comes!" Sal unfolded inside Buck's mouth and swelled like a water balloon. Buck saved the surprise for later and pulled back to only let the tip touch his tonsils. Sal's was by far the fattest cock he had ever sucked, and he might turn out to be the longest if the swelling continued, which it did. Sal's monster was in for a happy surprise, but right now, Buck pretended to be one of those dumb amateurs who use two hands and just lick the tip. He looked up at Sal's disappointed face, chuckling to himself.

Sal complained, "Is that all you got? I -- hey!"

Buck knew how to use his skill and also when to use it. In one swift motion, he unhinged his jaw and opened his esophagus, going all the way down until his face was buried in Sal's pubes. He wasn't sure how long he could keep it up, but he wouldn't stop until Sal was impressed.

Sal saw the boy inhale his Italian salami like it was an aspirin. The shock of being fully engulfed by this boy's mouth and throat was a sensation he had never believed possible, not since he hit puberty. That's when he watched his friends grow taller while he just saw all the added inches go to his cock. It put him in a class apart, the well-hung. His former friends teased him mercilessly, whinnying like horses whenever he passed by. In addition to the perfect, impossible blow job, Sal felt an odd sensation behind his eyes. It was emotion. His eyes were shedding tears of self-pity, joy, and pleasure. He quickly wiped them away and stuffed his feelings deeper than Buck could stuff Sal's cock. He leaned back, letting in only pleasure.

The burning and stretching were unlike anything Buck had endured in his throat. But looking up at Sal, head thrown back in ecstasy, he knew he had to keep at it. Sal deserved to know how it felt to be balls to chin with an expert cocksucker. Mercifully, Sal didn't buck or thrust. He let Buck take charge and perform his job with expert timing. Like a long-distance swimmer, Buck pulled back for oxygen every three or four strokes.

Sal was an ass man. He had met a few guys in his life who could take it. They were rare. He gazed at Buck's perky ass and wondered if he was one of those rare talents. He had already left Sal dumbfounded by his oral talents. But the truth was that Sal considered a blow job, no matter how expert, foreplay for the real deal.

Buck's eyes were watering. His throat burned from all the gagging and stretching. So it came as a huge relief when Sal asked hesitantly, "You—you like to…take it up the ass"?

Buck extracted Sal's meat from his throat, inch by inch until he got the whole fat mess out of his mouth so he could talk. "Hell, yes!"

In moments, the arrangement changed. Sal hoisted Buck's knees up, then situated the lower legs over his shoulders. Sal's big spongy dick was perfectly poised at the entrance. Buck reached under his bed for his satchel and took out a big tub of dime-store petroleum jelly. "We are gonna need this."

Sal applied the jelly liberally to his cock, then worked a glob up into Buck's crack. He worked one finger, then two into Buck. He didn't protest; he just wriggled and grinned with anticipation.

Buck loved to get fucked. Usually, his fat cock attracted, then frightened away the size-hungry men, who fled without giving him so much as a hand job. In the army, Buck had discovered that his ass drove men wild so long as he could disguise his thick meat. He wore jock straps to keep his dick pressed tight, and the ass fuckers took notice. His creamy white butt cheeks drew them in, quietly, at first, so the other guys didn't know. He spent many hours lying quietly on his side, taking a long line of horny night visitors inside him. Then word got around. The army was a melting pot where all manner of men collided. Tall, short, skinny, fat, muscular, puny, big dick, or little dick. They all had one thing in common: they needed to get off. And Buck was one of the lucky men who got off by letting other guys get off inside him. He had sucked and swallowed and had taken it in the ass from a whole platoon, one soldier at a time. Then the sadistic CO wanted in on the action exclusively. He was one of the hypocrites who threw him out when he was caught in the act.

But all that fucking had taught him how to please a man of any size. Sal was probably not the biggest, but so much sex happened under a wool army blanket in the dark, so he wasn't sure. He had definitely never seen one that looked so big.

By now, Sal had four fingers and a thumb in Buck, preparing him for the elephant trunk to come. Buck wore a smile of anticipation, something Sal hadn't seen before. Most men were trembling with fear. Buck reached out and held the tip of Sal's cock steady while he scooted forward on the bed, pressing his pink hole against the giant, throbbing manhood. Sal licked his lips.

"Just do it, man," Buck begged.

Hearing these words made even more blood flow into his cock, so he was fully, impossibly huge. Still, he believed it was unlikely that Buck's eagerness would last long, and soon enough, Sal would have to pull out and jack off. He underestimated Buck's strength and experience. The first inch went in easily. There was a pop as his corona passed the gates. Buck was still smiling with no fear. What a brave boy. Three more inches, and Sal was getting to the point where even the most courageous men always gave up. Not Buck.

Buck craned his neck and watched the cook press his meat deep inside. With his legs over his shoulders, he shouldn't have been able to see Sal's cock, but it was so big that even four inches in, there remained an enviable length of cock waiting to enter. Buck adjusted, sliding another inch of Sal inside him. Now he started to feel the burn he rarely felt anymore.

Sal saw Buck wince for the first time. "You okay"?

Buck grunted, "Let you know if I ain't. Keep going."

Sal was really impressed with the boy. There was

still a long way to go. Inch by inch, Sal forced himself deeper into Buck. He reached the bottom, the place where the rectum ends and the sigmoid colon begins. For a majority of receptive men, like Mike, for instance, this is the end of the ride. If your man is too big, like Sal, he can't push further without tearing or damaging tissue. But some men are built a little differently. The sigmoid is flexible and moveable. A horse-hung man can press and push past this junction with these talented guys. Buck was in the latter category. He had no trouble adjusting his angle to let Sal slide by. Buck was built to give men pleasure, and he knew it. He looked up at Sal's delighted face and spoke. "I want all of it. Now."

With a final thrust, Sal invaded Buck fully. Sal's hips were resting against Buck's buttocks. Buck knew Sal had even more to give. Like a circus acrobat, Buck rotated onto his side until his outstretched legs formed a right angle, giving Sal complete access to his hole. And Sal went for it. His cock slid in another half inch, and it was all the way in. His pubic mound rested against Buck's anal opening. Buck reached around Sal and pulled his ass closer, so the club-like cock would go a few centimeters more.

"How do you want it, Buck? Long and slow, or fast and deep"?

"I want you to pump that giant all the way in and out."

"So...long and slow."

Buck nodded but then added, "Slow at first, maybe. But you can go fast real soon." And that is precisely what happened. Sal arched his back to extract 90% of his cock, slowly pushing his way back deep inside Buck. Buck didn't gripe, made no complaint, only moaned softly under his breath, releasing stuttering sighs of pleasure with each stroke and the occasional gasp when Sal bumped the bottom before finding the gateway to his sigmoid colon.

Sal picked up the pace, and the soft moans became muted grunts of pleasure. Buck was a pig for Sal's mammoth meat. So Sal started feeding the little pig faster and faster. Buck squealed and writhed under Sal, who now held both ankles wide apart, entering Buck from the front so he could watch his face twitch.

And twitch it did. Despite himself, Buck started to feel the kind of pain that cannot easily give any pleasure. Sal was being rough, maybe too rough, but Buck was determined to take all of him, right to the end. So he made those facial contortions into a smile.

Buck added, for good measure, "Holy shit can you fuck!"

Sal didn't know why, but he smacked Buck hard across the face and said, "And you love it, you little whore."

Both men gazed at each other in surprise. That slap was a massive turn-on for both of them. Sal slapped him three or four times; he lost count. Buck cried out, but Sal didn't care anymore. He pounded deep, fast, and hard, challenging Buck to take it like the man who bragged he could.

Real tears formed in Buck's eyes and rolled down his cheeks. But his cock was rock hard, despite so many kinds of pain. He held on to his erect member with one hand, stroking it rhythmically to match Sal's rapid thrusts. He clawed at the sheets and blankets with the other hand, then pounded his fists on the bed to keep his mind off the crippling pain.

Sal wanted to feel bad for the kid, but he felt too good. He had not fucked with wild abandon ever, not ever in his whole life, and Buck was the first to let him go hard, fast, and past the rectum. He felt like he could do this for hours.

Buck needed it to end soon, or he might never walk again. He took his free hand and cupped Sal's balls, using one finger to tickle the perineal ridge near his anus.

Sal was not prepared for this touch. It didn't startle him; it pushed him over the precipice. He wanted to fuck the kid for hours, but now there were only seconds left.

Buck smiled to himself. He knew most men better than they knew themselves. In desperation, he taught himself this trick with one massive, very rough soldier. The minute he wanted to end it, he pressed that seam, and Old Faithful erupted.

Buck was extremely turned on. It was not often he was rock hard with such a massive cock inside him. He usually dribbled soft like D. But this was different. It was as if every crevice, every fold of his insides, were stretched and quivering. It wouldn't be long now.

Sal thrust like a jackrabbit, letting out guttural bursts as he approached climax. He looked down to see Buck, eyes closed, smiling, jacking his own meat. There was a spot on Buck's trim belly where Sal's huge cock came close to the surface, forming a protruding bulge with each deep thrust. Sal put his hand there and could feel his dick sliding inside Buck like a little baby kicking its mother. He lost it.

Sal spasmed and shuddered as he shot his load deep into Buck's guts. He had no idea how much semen he'd planted inside the boy.

Buck felt Sal gushing into him past his rectum. There was a warm, flooding sensation in his colon. He'd thought he was all spent from his earlier encounter with D, but the extremes of sensation he'd just endured had cleared the slate. Sal stayed planted inside Buck but licked at his balls and cockshaft. Buck jerked himself towards climax.

Within moments, Buck started taking shallower breaths. He blew air through his nostrils and grunted like a pig.

"Shoot, little piggy." Sal coaxed him to come.

Sal grew softer inside Buck, and his length and girth decreased slowly at first, then more rapidly. Buck felt the beast shrink, then slide. It was that sensation, the natural slithering movement, coupled with the ever-increasing relief from pain, that brought Buck to the precipice. There was so much dick inside him that, even soft, it filled his rectum with soft, spongy flesh. Buck bore down and shit Sal's dick out.

As the head came out and Buck's gaping hole gently closed, the flood of relief became a fountain of sperm. It shot past Buck's ear and splattered on the headboard. A second spray landed on his mouth and chin. Four or five more bursts landed progressively closer to their source.

In the afterglow, Sal picked up his distended softie and dropped it on Buck's crotch. Even soft, Sal was double the volume of Buck, who was still stiff with the vigor of youth. Buck put his palm on the instrument of his near destruction and rolled it like a rolling pin from side to side on his belly.

"See, I told you I could take you," he taunted Sal.

Sal chuckled, saying, "Either way, I was gonna be the winner."

And so he was.

5

SMOKE RINGS

Sal and Buck worked doubly fast to make up for lost time. The dishes were drying; the beds were made (and wiped down, in one case), and both men had a sponge bath to remove the evidence of their liaison. But Buck was limping. He wasn't injured, just really banged up inside. This is what his first and only girlfriend meant when she said, "After that, I couldn't walk straight for a week." That was her breakup line, in fact. Buck had probably been with a few guys that were as long as Sal or maybe as thick, but not both; Sal was his first truly huge cock. He limped as he cleaned and winced when he sat down to tie his shoes.

He wasn't fooling anyone. When the guys returned from the barn, they repressed chuckles as they watched him hobble from one side of the room to the other.

Mike stepped up to address the obvious. "From what I can see, you probably lasted longer than any of us with Sal."

Buck saw the futility in protesting or denying the obvious, so he merely nodded in agreement.

Sal piped up, "He's got stamina and talent. He runs circles around you amateurs. He let me go so long that I came inside him."

The various looks that Buck got were a menagerie of emotions. Amazement, jealousy, self-doubt...

Mike was jealous. He pouted. He thought about his long thin dick and how easy it would be to fuck Buck if Sal could do it. He was angry with Sal for taking Buck without his permission. Mike didn't own Buck, but he was Top Dog in the bunkhouse and had certain rights.

D was dumbfounded. His captor this morning was so dominant; how could he flip so quickly? And how could he take such a gargantuan piece of meat for more than a minute? D could never get started with Sal; he was just too ridiculously big. Bear was even longer than Sal but pretty narrow at the tip. D had learned to take him briefly, and if he had enough beer, he could go a little deeper. That was it. Buck was Superman.

Will Dewey stroked his chin and thought how nice it would be to hold Buck. He wondered if the boy had ever been with an older man.

Bear was eager to get his paws on the boy and deep-dick him. He rarely met a man who could handle more than the first few inches. They ended up giving him a fake blowjob with two hands and a very full mouth. Judging by how the boy was limping, Bear knew in his heart that he would have to give it a few days. But he didn't want to wait, and he had a plan.

It was shower time. Mike went first. Buck was last, and with all the hot water gone, he shivered under the cold spray, letting it run down the crack of his ass in a cooling stream.

Sal had prepared an Italian minestrone with garlic bread. He served Buck last to maintain the pecking order. He slipped Buck an extra wedge of Garlic bread under the table but said nothing. Buck was grateful for the kindness. Sal was thankful for Buck's sexual expertise, which finally allowed him to feel like a normal man, not a circus freak.

D offered to help Sal wash up so Buck was free to

join the guys for a smoke. The summer air was humid and balmy. Buck couldn't imagine what winter would be like in a drafty old bunkhouse. He had a pretty good idea of how the men stayed warm.

They broke out a couple of six-packs of Lucky Lager, and Mike fired up a joint. Buck eagerly took the beer but looked askance at the weed when it came around. Will nudged him. "Go on. It helps with aches and pains."

Buck caught Will's meaning and drew in a heavy breath of smoke. Immediately he began coughing. He chewed and smoked tobacco, but weed was new for him.

Mike winked conspiratorially, saying, "Buck, you blew it all away. Try again, gently. And hold it in."

Buck took another toke, held it in, then slowly released a trail of pot smoke. To show off, he blew a couple of smoke rings.

"I don't feel anything different," he said.

Mike had a sadistic sense of humor. "You probably didn't get enough; try again."

Will started to protest, but Mike stared him into silence. He watched as Buck sucked in another intoxicating blast, chased it with a swig of beer, and blew out the smoke, gently coughing.

Buck looked around at Mike, Bear, and Will. He felt like he had sprouted hummingbird wings and was hovering about 3 inches above the ground. He could hear the wings fluttering. Mike was snickering quietly.

"He's as stoned as Saint Stephen."

"Get him a chair."

"Here, boy, sit down." Will was the kindly man who brought him a humble footstool.

Buck plopped down hard in the chair and let out a yelp of pain.

Bear and Mike laughed uproariously, but Will remained serious. He squatted down so he could talk to Buck at eye level.

Buck gazed into Will's eyes. They were two emerald pools surrounded by snowy mountains.

"Hey, Buck, this is your first time getting stoned, isn't it?"

Buck nodded and reached toward Will's face. He rubbed his hands across Will's snowy eyebrows and said, "Gray makes better hay."

Will let Buck explore his face. He recalled his youth when he first smoked a marijuana cigarette with his brother's friends. His brother wasn't there to protect him from what came next.

But tonight, Will remained with Buck. He knew how important a trustworthy friend could be. Not that Mike and Bear were untrustworthy, they just weren't very kind. Buck needed kindness.

Like a mind reader, Buck poked Will in the shoulder and said, "You, sir, are a very kind man. Hey, where's my beer?" Buck searched in vain. He had finished it already, and no more was coming. He reached for Will's hand and squeezed it, holding it close to his heart.

"I like you, Will. I do. We only just met, but I can tell you're good people."

Mike and Bear wandered back inside, leaving the two men alone under the stars.

Will didn't talk; he just listened to the boy ramble, nodding in agreement with whatever he said. In a few minutes, Buck was sound asleep. Will summoned Bear, who carried the sleeping lad to his bed.

Together they removed his boots and coat and covered him. Buck curled up in a fetal position and put his thumb in his mouth. Will and Bear exchanged glances, agreeing to leave Buck and his thumb-sucking out of future conversations.

6

BEAR

The following day, Buck awoke sore, dizzy, and disoriented. He had no memory of going to bed. He always slept in the nude, but he was fully dressed. He saw his boots standing beside a stool that held his neatly folded coat.

The events of the previous night came to him in bits and pieces. He remembered drinking under the stars, smoking weed, and talking to Will. He remembered Mike gave him the weed and laughed at him when he fell into a chair. After that, it went dark.

No matter. It was before dawn on a new day, and there was work to do. After breakfast, D and Buck gingerly mounted their horses, each man wincing in pain from the ass fucking they had taken the day before. They rode drag together. This time Buck was lead so D could observe his technique. He did well, and D let him know it. Under the scrub oak, D sucked off the new recruit for a job well done. Buck was grateful for the reward and returned the favor, despite his sore, scratchy throat, still in recovery from Mike and Sal.

Riding drag meant breathing a lot of dust. Buck didn't mind. We all start somewhere.

The supper bell rang out as the team brought the cattle back to the corral. The hard-working cowboys hungrily downed their beef stew, but Buck sipped and swallowed slowly. Mike noticed and felt compelled to comment.

"Was I too much for you"?

Buck shook his head and pointed to Sal. "He was."

The whole crew broke out laughing except Mike. Steam came out of his ears. He reached across the table and smacked Buck so hard his lip began bleeding.

"Mike, leave the boy alone!" His whole crew was glaring at him. He felt his top dog status threatened by the new arrival. He knew his cock was no destroyer like Sal's, but Buck had driven the point home.

He knew what he needed to do. "Sorry, kid, I was out of line. I know you meant me no lack of respect."

"Oh, gosh, no, Mike. You was right. I spoke out of turn."

"You spoke the truth, and there's no crime in that. Here, let me get that." Mike dabbed at the boy's split lip.

After Mike finished wiping the blood from his lip, Buck broke out with a charming smile. He knew the power structure and where he belonged. Mike ruled the bunkhouse, and he needed to command respect. They all had their place in the pack.

After lunch, Bear asked to borrow Buck in the barn. A cow was calving, but she needed some help. Buck had never attended a birth. He wasn't sure he could stomach it. But it was all in the job.

In the barn, Bear pointed out the tools they might need. He picked up a plastic bottle filled with a clear liquid.

"This is O B Lube. It's our magic bullet."

"What's it do?"

"You'll see soon enough because I need your skinny little arms for this job."

Bear held up his giant hands and rolled down his sleeves to reveal massive forearms.

"I can't go in there with these mitts; I would tear a hole in her lady parts."

As if the cow spoke English, she mooed in agreement.

"I cain't tell what we're doing; I'm sorry, sir."

Bear sighed. "I thought you were a farmer. Ain't you never birthed a calf?"

Buck admitted his ignorance.

"Well, here's the deal: the calf is stuck, and you're gonna put your pretty little arms up there and pull that calf out."

Buck suppressed a gag and coolly said, "Sounds easy enough."

Bear continued. "This lube is so slick; it would let you drive a tank up a gnat's ass. So you should take off your shirt. O B gets everywhere if you're not careful."

Buck stripped to the waist. Bear eyed the young man's proportions with lust and envy. He poured a small puddle of O B lube into Buck's cupped palms. "Okay, now spread it up and down your arms. "

Buck did as he was told. The liquid was the slickest substance he had ever felt. If he needed to pick something up now, he wouldn't be able to.

"Hey, Bear, how am I gonna hold onto the calf?"

"O B Lube lets you reach around the calf and pull it from behind. Use your fingers like hooks. Got it? Good. Now go gently; go deep. That's my motto."

Buck heard the double entendre, but he was concentrating on the job. Against loud vocal protests from the mother, he entered the cow and found the calf wedged inside. Just as promised, he easily slid his hands along the uterine wall around the calf. Curling his fingers into hooks, he locked onto the calf and pulled. There was no movement. He pulled again, and the cow let out a scream.

"Wait!" Bear grabbed a spray bottle containing a

clear oily liquid and sprayed it liberally inside the cow. "Mineral oil. She must have dried out. Try again."

Buck pulled and felt movement. It reminded him of that magic moment when he knows his cock is going to get past the hump and all the way in.

Blood and mucus coated his chest and stained his jeans. The calf's exit accelerated. Buck lost his footing and fell back, clutching the calf to his chest. He felt his ribs nearly crack from the weight as the wind was taken from him. He fainted. When he came to, Bear was washing the newborn in a sink. The cow stood over Buck, licking his face.

Outside, the two men shared a menthol cigarette. Buck hated menthol, but he needed a smoke after that ordeal. Plus, menthol was good for you.

"Did I do okay"? He was worried he had messed up.

"Kid, the cow is alive, the calf is alive, and nobody is bleeding to death. You did good."

Buck beamed at the praise.

"It's a job I just can't do. Here, let me see your hand." Buck held up his hand, and Bear pressed their palms together. The giant man's hand was a major league catcher's mitt, and Buck's was the hand of a little league player.

"Now let me see your arm."

Bear took Buck's arm by the wrist and compared it against his. This was how he planned to make his move.

"Your arm is three times as thick as mine."

"Yeah, like I said, I could never do what you just did. Being big is a blessing and a curse."

Buck nodded, thinking of Sal.

"Let me see your leg," Bear asked. They compared legs with similar results. Buck was shorter and less muscular than Bear. It was confirmed. Not really front-page news.

Out of the corner of his eye, he caught some movement. Bear was rubbing his massive hand up and down his left pant leg. In perfect relief, Buck could see the giant cock straining against the fabric. In an instant, Buck had an erection of his own. He wasn't sure where this was going, but he liked it so far.

"Buck, I bet I am bigger than you in every way."

"Yeah?" Buck had a card up his sleeve he hadn't revealed. "In every way, you say? What do you wager?"

"Loser gets fucked."

Buck still felt bruised and used. He was sure his cock was thicker, but he wasn't sure he could stand to be wrong. Still, he heard himself say, "I'll take that bet."

Bear chuckled. It wasn't a fair deal, but the boy took it.

They headed back to the barn, where Bear produced a cloth tape measure.

Buck watched greedily as Bear kept lowering his jeans, revealing more and impossibly more of his long, thick cock. It wasn't quite as thick as Sal's, but it was clearly much longer. The effect was intoxicating. Given all the cocks in the bunkhouse, Sal's looked the biggest due to optical illusion, but Bear had the greatest volume by far. It was a flesh baseball bat.

"Buck, you think you got more than this?" Bear wasn't even fully hard yet.

"Get it good and hard, 'cause I think I got you beat."

Bear pulled his flesh fuck stick out of his jeans and jerked it a few times. His cock grew longer and longer still, but not any thicker. He placed the end of the tape measure at the base of his cock and rolled it out triumphantly to a place over which only a handful of men in the world had bragging rights. Over 10 inches. People bragged about ten-inch dicks, but nobody had one. Except for Bear.

Buck was astonished. It was now officially the biggest dick he had ever seen. But not the thickest.

"Okay, now go around the widest part. Let's see how

big around you are."

Bear obliged. "6 and 3/16, pretty goddamn big." He grinned and said, "There is no way you are even close to ten inches."

Buck feigned defeat, then said, "Let me see that tape measure."

He pulled out his six-and-a-half-inch cock, and Bear laughed. He wasn't humiliating Buck, but he was definitely giving him shit.

Bear handed over the measure, and Buck found the part of his cock that scared off so many men. He carefully circled his cock at the widest point. Seven-and-a-half. Buck grinned. "I beat you."

"The fuck you did! I'm nearly four inches longer than you."

"You bet that you could beat me in every way. I'm way thicker than you."

"You ain't fucking me,"

"Then you ain't fucking me. I won the wager you made fair and square."

Bear grinned, "I'll tell you what, Buck. I will fuck you on length; you can fuck me on width."

Buck paled, thinking of the horrific beating his insides took yesterday from Sal.

"Does it have to be today?"

Bear thought about it, but then he said, "Yep."

"I am one big bruise up in there. You'll kill me."

"If you fall off one horse, pick yourself up and get back on...this horse." Bear pointed to his swollen member, which throbbed and pulsated with anticipation.

Buck admitted to himself that this would be an excellent time to train for what he knew would be a nonstop barrage of huge hungry cocks all year long. He could get his sea legs, so to speak, by taking on Bear today.

With a shrug, Buck knelt down and put the head of the immense cock in his mouth.

"Hey, hey. Nobody can suck me off. It's not poss--"

Bear gasped in amazement as Buck unhinged his jaw and let him into his mouth. He figured that was going to be it, a hand job disguised as a blow job in lieu of a painful, glorious assfucking. Buck had two hands on Bear's exposed shaft, pretending once more he was like the girl who didn't know how to suck dick properly. He smiled inwardly, planning for the surprise. The truth is, once you figure out how to let a giant cock pass your tonsils and enter the esophagus, it really makes no difference how long or thick it is. They all fit eventually.

Bear grumbled, "I don't like getting head. The teeth, and it's--"

Buck knew this was the right moment. He let his epiglottis relax, then inhaled the enormous meat in one go. Buck looked up to see Bear moan with the sublime joy of getting deep-throated for the first time in his life.

Buck found he could avoid an ass fucking if he kept this up for much longer, but he knew it wasn't fair. A deal's a deal, and he needed to jump on that horse dick to fulfill his part of the bargain.

He reared back, letting the entire length of Bear's cock exit his throat and flop out of his mouth. It was covered in spit, but Buck didn't think he could manage it in his ass now that it was laid out before him.

But then Bear reached up to the shelf and brought down the bottle of O B Lube. He grinned at Buck and said, "This O B lube has many uses." He put a small amount of the incredibly slippery substance on his cock and gestured for Buck to lay face down across a saddle on a nearby saw horse. Bear was still recovering from the shock of going down Buck's throat. He was thrilled to see Buck so compliant as he bent over the saddle, exposing a perfect pink butthole surrounded by two white mounds of flesh and peach fuzz. If it was possible, Bear got even harder.

Buck bared his ass to this hairy beast and feared the

worst. He wished he could take a painkiller or a diet pill before letting the monster invade his inner sanctum.

But then, to Buck's surprise, Bear slipped into him with barely a pinch of pain. The O B Lube created a frictionless barrier that slipped past his suffering sphincter and filled his rectum with throbbing meat. Bear was an expert at ass fucking. He reached the end of the rectum and deftly slipped his entire length into Buck, invading several inches of his colon. He waited there, allowing Buck to adjust.

"You okay, boy"?

Buck nodded in surprise. Despite the brutal fuck he took yesterday from Sal, taking Bear was more effortless and even more pleasurable. Bear retreated a few inches, then buried himself deep inside the boy again.

Buck felt Bear's fur rubbing against his bare legs. It was wiry and rough. He arched his back to connect his shoulders with the man's furry chest. He hoped that someday he would have some hair on his chest. But now, it was only a few wisps of curly hairs near his nipples.

Bear slid in and out easily because the obstetric lube brought friction to near zero. Buck was talented at taking cock. The ease and grace with which he accepted Bear inside him was a testament to the boy's skill and military training. He may be the best fuck he ever had.

"Turn around, boy, and put your back on the saddle. don't worry; I got you." Bear held his ankles tightly while he wriggled into a modified missionary position.

From this angle, he could see Bear pull back far, farther than any ordinary man could go without popping out, and then plunge in so the hairy man's hips were pressed firmly against his buttocks. Buck rubbed his invader's belly hair, then sniffed his fingers, taking in the intoxicating scent of male primal lust.

Bear saw this and knew the boy wanted to be closer. In one deft movement, he hoisted Buck astride his hips and held him close. Buck moaned with pleasure, feeling the whole hairy torso pressed against his hairless upper body. Invisible sparks of desire crackled between them, bringing each a little closer to climax. Bear carried the young man around the barn, sliding the tender ass up and down his meaty pole. Then Bear gently set him back on the saddle so he could focus his strength on rutting. Buck held back, wanting to be fully erect when it was time to flip. He wanted to give Bear a full load.

Bear marveled at the new guy's talents. He rarely met a man who could take part of him, let alone his whole fat, long cock. The average rectum is only about four inches long. Over the years, Bear found a few eager guys who could take his girth, but he always bottomed out with them. They weren't skilled enough to allow a long cock to turn the corner. It was for this reason that he usually was on the bottom. He could take a dick and enjoy it. Being so huge, his asshole was very accommodating. He had never seen a cock like Buck's with that club-like wide spot. He shrugged and guessed it would be easy, given how short it was. Then Bear again turned his attention back to Buck, who was taking one for the team.

Buck was extremely aroused, and it was all he could do to keep from coming hands-free. Bear was a huge furry animal, pounding ever more intensely into his guts. Buck was proud of his ability to turn pain into pleasure. It reminded him of the weight room back at the barracks, where he learned to lift weights through the burn, which was always worse the second day. He learned a lot in that weight room. He would never be here today, in this musty barn, taking the hugest dick of his life, were it not for the training he received from his army buddies. But he had to shift his focus back to giving Bear a good ride.

Bear felt the stirrings of a climax in his belly. He looked down and watched his cock disappear completely inside Buck. It was arousing. It made Bear feel powerful and talented, using the gift nature gave him to stretch this young man to his limits. The rush of power and domination was making him lightheaded. Maybe it was all the blood draining from his brain into his dick, but it was an incredible high. Buck looked into Bear's eyes and moaned, "fuck me, Bear."

Those three words multiplied his sense of power and domination. He was deep inside this young man who wanted him there enough to beg for it. Bear saw stars just before his floodgates opened, filling Buck from stem to stern with buttery white hot ejaculate. He pulled out his still-shooting cock and sprayed Buck on his downy soft butt cheeks. Buck was so well-fucked, his anus gaped open, exposing Bear's handiwork inside the boy. The cum mingled with the sticky lube, leaking a pale sticky stream of fuck juice onto the sawdust-covered barn floor. Bear lifted his still-hard member and plunged it quickly inside the well-fucked chute. Buck groaned with pleasure. His cock was at full attention. Bear stayed inside the boy, feeling the river of lube and cum damming behind his flesh barricade. When he pulled out quickly, the suction brought a torrent of semen and lubricant. Buck cupped his hand and held some in reserve.

Buck grinned and said, "Your turn." Bear helped Buck down off the saddle.

"I was gonna say the same thing."

The men looked around the barn for a suitable place to fuck. Buck wasn't tall enough to reach Bear on the saddle or standing up, for that matter.

Buck didn't want to lose his hard-on, so he slicked up his cock with the O B Lube and the cum from his cupped hand. He slowly jerked his meat until it was slippery all up and down the length.

"Get on all fours," Buck ordered sternly.

Bear laughed good-naturedly, then locked eyes with

Buck. He was deadly serious.

"You fucked me hard; I'm gonna fuck you like an animal."

Bear liked this game. He got on all fours and parted his thighs, revealing a tight pink butthole in a whirlpool of fur, framed by hairy butt cheeks, his pendulous cock dragging close to the ground.

"I don't want to be gentle," Buck breathed. "You ready for me now"?

Bear had no time to protest or answer. In a flash, Buck had his little cock head inside Bear, and he plowed in right to his hips. He had loved every second of the brutal fuck Bear had given him, but he wanted to hurt him back. Not out of cruelty but out of dignity. He had earned the right to turn it around.

And indeed, Bear yelped in pain as the wine-bottle-thick part of Buck's ovoid manhood popped past his sphincter. And Buck didn't let up. He pulled and pushed the thickest part of his cock past Bear's tight ring, sending waves of pain shooting through his ass. He wanted so badly to beg Buck to stop, but that would mean he was the bigger pussy.

Buck grinned with pleasure watching spontaneous tears of pain form in the corners of the eyes of his 'cattle.' He owned Bear right now. He wanted to brand him, to say, "This ass is mine." But it was a fleeting desire.

By now, Bear had gotten used to Buck's brutal thick spot and started to like it. The hairy man's pendulous cock lifted away from the floor but was too long and heavy to reach his hanging belly. The flashes of pain became like a rhythmic electric pulse. As Bear relaxed, he resisted the man less. His ass was used to the boy now.

Buck felt disappointment, knowing that his cock couldn't brutalize Bear in the same way. Bear was big everywhere, even his asshole. So Buck took things up a notch.

Coating his hand with O B Lube, he slipped out of

Bear, then formed a four-finger spear out of his fist. He pushed the furry hole and started to press in.

Bear bucked like a bull. "Hey, we didn't talk about fists!"

Buck responded with a sadistic grin, "That's right. We didn't."

Bear could turn around and deck this kid with very little effort.

"Unless, of course, you aren't man enough to take my tiny little fist up your huge fuckhole."

Bear knew the psychological game Buck was playing and decided to give in.

"On one condition," he asked, "lube me up good."

Buck squirted the bottle of O B Lube up inside the beast of a man. His hand slid in part way, despite moans of discomfort from the man on all fours. The O B Lube was so slick it would be very easy to punch into the man right now, but Buck knew he would get more pleasure and less blood if he took things slowly. He began thrusting his arm forward in a rhythmic motion. Each thrust got his hand a little further in until he reached the widest part of his hand that traversed the thumb and pinky. Here he stayed, pushing gently, gently, until his whole hand slipped by Bear's anal ring. The sphincter snapped shut on his wrist. Gently, Buck pulled his hand back towards him, causing Bear to pound the sawdust and howl.

"Am I hurting you"? Buck asked innocently.

Bear would never give him the pleasure of seeing him break. He shook his head and, in a painful whisper, gasped, "It feels so fucking good."

Buck grinned wickedly and pulled his hand out with a popping sound softened only by the wet slurps of O B Lube. Immediately, he plunged his hand back in, up to his wrist. After a couple more cruel entries and exits, Buck began the business he had planned from the start.

"We got a problem, Bear."

"We do"?

"Yes," Buck confirmed. I've got a cow, and there's something up the birth canal that needs to be manipulated."

Bear knew he was the cow, but what else besides Buck's fist required manual removal?

In answer to his question, Bear felt blinding white hot pain as Buck began slipping his cock past his wrist, up inside the man.

Bear whimpered and tried to cover it up with a satisfied moan.

Buck stopped. "I'm not hurting you, am I? I can always stop. Just say the word."

Bear's pride trumped his pain. He adamantly shook his head no.

Buck pulled his hand out far enough to grasp the tip of his dick, then pushed forward, pulling his thick tool inside the already-stuffed man.

Buck kept sliding and adjusting until his cock was firmly in his hand up inside Bear.

"The only way to get this breech birth of a cock out is to get it to shoot a load."

Bear grunted, adjusting and adapting to the pain with surprising ease. This was a day of firsts for him. First deep throat, first hip-to-ass penetration balls deep, and now the first time a man had his fist and his cock inside him at the same time.

Buck began stroking his cock inside the man. He had heard whispers of the taboo practice of fist-jacking, but he had never seen or tried it. It was satisfying hearing the cries of pain emanating from the monster he was fucking. He wanted Bear to cry uncle, but it wasn't happening.

Bear could feel Buck jerking his thick cock inside him. His guts were stretched in various directions as Buck yanked his meat in a frenzy. He hazarded a question, "Is that calf still stuck"?

"It's loosening," Buck answered. And it was. Buck was not going to be able to hold back for long. His strokes were tight and effective in the cramped flesh chamber where they were jammed. He looked down at Bear, bravely taking a fist and a fat dick at the same time. Despite what must be blinding pain, his soft moans sounded like pleasure. His giant dangling cock was leaking clear fluid. Buck reached down with his free hand and let a few drops of the precious liquid spill onto his finger. He licked it lovingly, surprised by the strong, manly taste.

The pre-ejaculate was the last straw. Buck was jacking too fast to move back from the edge. He stopped and waited for the wave of pleasure to disperse so he could continue, but it didn't. Maybe it was the taste of Bear's seminal fluid or the sight and sound of this massive hunk moaning while taking him on all fours, but the combinations of scents, tastes, sights, and sensations threw Buck over the edge.

He pulled out very suddenly, causing Bear to suppress a scream. He jacked his semen all over the man's gaping butthole.

Bear felt the warm goo basting his hairy ass. He was so turned on he shot another load on the floor without touching himself. Then he felt Buck slip his softening cock back into his hole.

"Round two"? He asked greedily.

Buck shook his head and emitted a sigh. Bear felt hot liquid filling his rectum and then his colon.

Buck was letting loose a gushing stream of urine inside Bear. He had not relieved himself all day. The piss filled Bear and deepened his humiliation. Buck felt like he'd won the contest. Bear ran to the toilet to empty his bowels.

Buck cleaned the O B Lube off his ass and put his clothes back on. He returned to the bunkhouse for a thorough shower.

❦ 7 ❧

DICK

Back at the bunkhouse, a stranger was inspecting the beds. Buck was surprised when the man whirled around and grinned. He was handsome, like how James Dean might have looked if he hadn't been in that car crash in California. The cocky man extended his hand and said, "You must be Buck. I'm Dick Burns, the owner of this ranch."

Buck shook his hand and smiled, "Right, you hired me."

He looked at Buck's O B Lube-soaked clothes. "Breech birth"?

"Yep, but I got it out."

"Good man." Dick moved past him, apparently disinterested, and continued his tour of the digs.

Dick Burns had never seen someone as handsome as Buck. It was all he could do to keep from drooling. It didn't help that the boy was making doe eyes at him. Dick was a handsome ranch owner, and he knew it. He had a particular effect on men...and women. But he didn't live in the Big Hole River Valley because he wanted to marry a woman. This was man's country through and through.

"Don't let me keep you from washing up."

Buck nodded and walked obediently to the showers.

He didn't bother closing the door, as always. The guys had no reason to be shy around one another. He looked down at his jeans and his t-shirt. Both were covered in lube and the calve's amniotic fluids. They were pretty bad. Later he would take them to the river and wash them. For now, he folded them and put his boots on top. The shower floor grew slick as he cleaned the lube and other fluids from his body and asshole. O B Lube was everywhere, and soap had only a limited effect. You just had to keep diluting it with water and hope it drained away. Buck took a misstep, and his feet came out from under him. He felt his head hit the tile, and then his lights went out.

Dick heard a sharp crack from the shower room. He saw the handsome young man, unmoving, laid out like a patient on a table. Dick rushed in and almost lost his footing on the slick floor. He turned off the spigots and knelt to take Buck's pulse. His heartbeat was strong, and he was breathing. Good.

He picked up the naked, unconscious Buck in his arms and carried him to his bunk. He laid him out and covered his lower body with a sheet.

Buck awoke in his bunk to the smiling face of Dick Burns.

"You whacked your head pretty bad, son. Must be that goddamn O B Lube. You gotta use salt to get it off."

Buck nodded, "It's very slippery, sir."

Dick felt an automatic stirring in his loins when this young Adonis called him 'sir.'

"And you, son, are very lucky." He winked.

"Yes, sir."

There it was again, the blue-eyed boy calling him 'sir.'

Buck's eyes were blurry at first, but they came to focus on Dick's crotch. He saw it jump each time he called him 'sir.' He was having a similar reaction to being called 'son.'. The sheet couldn't hide it anymore. Buck's cock was ballooning between his legs.

Dick saw the growing mass and rubbed his chin. He was also getting hard now. It was more than a mere stirring. Buck reached for Dick's crotch and stroked the outline of his cock. It felt like a can of Coca-Cola.

"Sir, is this why they call you Dick Burns"?

Dick laughed heartily, nodding yes. "Son, you have to be very experienced to handle a beer can cock. And it always burns."

"I'll bet I can take it!" Buck boasted.

"I'll bet I can take it...what."

"Sir. I can take it, sir." Buck threw off the sheet and lifted his legs skyward, spreading his beautiful butt cheeks to expose his slightly worn but willing hole.

Dick needed no further invitation. He yanked down his jeans, his heavy cock springing to attention. He watched Buck for signs of fear or doubt. This was a brave cowboy. Dick parked his rotund cock head against the pink pucker. He spat on his finger and tested for resilience and friction by inserting it inside Buck to the last knuckle. It was incredibly slick.

"Is that O B Lube up there?"

"Yes, sir."

"You just might survive this," Dick boasted. He didn't want to ask how the lube got there or why. He had his suspicions, and that was enough. Dick's cock was exactly like a can of soda. It was a perfect cylinder from his pubes to the head. Only the rounded cock tip was not part of the cylinder. It was maybe a half inch of painless meat, followed by six inches of pure pain for any man or woman brave enough to try it. Dick didn't care if it hurt; he always fucked them whether they wanted it or not.

Dick pushed in the first half inch, meeting no resistance. This boy was talented.

"You good, son?"

Buck nodded. "Sir, yes, sir!"

Dick's cock swelled a little more at Buck's obedient compliance.

"Here comes the Burn," Dick shoved until he could get his massive girth past Buck's sphincter. In he went, an inch or two, and waited for Buck to scream to pull it out. He found it was best to pull out once or twice before ignoring the screams.

Buck was loose and sloppy, but Dick's thick monster stretched him tighter than he had imagined. He clawed at the sheets, feeling the notorious burn. He saw white lights dancing in front of his face. But Buck knew the game. Just wait, and it'll stop hurting. Dick asked him, "You need me to stop"?

"Sir, no sir!" And as he said it, Buck felt Dick grow a little harder inside him.

"Should I fuck you? You ain't gonna hear your farts for a week."

"Fuck me, sir."

Dick obliged, sliding right to the back of Buck's rectal cavity, filling and stretching it. "How you like that, son"?

"It burns, sir."

"What burns?"

"Your dick burns, sir."

"Exactly." And with that, Dick Burns began sliding back and forth like a locomotive, gathering speed gradually. He smiled down at Buck, whose rock-hard cock was dripping prostate juice. Dick knew he was fucking this tenderfoot right. It was so rare to find a man who enjoyed getting fucked like this.

Buck was in far more pain than he had planned, but it was all trumped by the ecstatic pleasure of being so thoroughly, evenly filled with Dick's manhood. And Dick had an instinctive urge to move in and out at ever-increasing speed, which was intoxicating. Anytime Buck wanted to feel even more burn, all he had to do was say, "Sir," and Dick would momentarily swell up to his maximum girth. It was an excruciating pleasure. It also seemed to bring Dick closer to climax.

Buck could have let Dick fuck him senseless for hours if they were alone. The team members would be walking in from their afternoon chores any minute. Plus, Buck was already pretty banged up inside and out; he didn't want to cripple himself. He began stroking himself and looking into Dick's eyes. He repeated his words softly, over and over. "Fuck me, sir, fuck me, sir."

Dick could not believe this young man. He was better than any woman or man he had ever fucked. He was so filled with lust that it made his cock even bigger. And it usually takes him hours to climax, but the blue-eyed man was so good, Dick was close. He started to grunt, locking eyes with Buck. His pounding slowed as Buck pounded his own meat faster.

Dick felt a warm flood of ecstasy build in his balls. It bubbled over and shot down his cock into Buck. He thoroughly basted Buck's insides with his white hot butter. He moaned and said, "Oh, yes, son."

Buck felt Dick climax. When he heard him call him son, it put him over the edge. He shot high in the air. A single massive glob of cum flew past Dick, narrowly missing the brim of his cowboy hat, and came to land on a blade of the ceiling fan. Buck breathed a sigh of relief as he felt Dick slide out, leaving his stretched and battered hole to recover from its multiple cock on-slaught.

WILL DEWEY

The bunkhouse door flew open, and Will Dewey strode in. Out of the corner of his eye, he detected motion in the bunks, so he went to investigate. Will saw Dick Burns putting his infamous log back into his jeans while Buck lay naked and exhausted on his bunk, too tired to care who saw him. Will cleared his throat.

"Hey, Dick! What brings you out to the bunkhouse?"

Dick looked up and smiled. "Will Dewey, Great to see you." Dick extended a hand stained with juices and O B Lube. He withdrew his hand with a sheepish grin. "Just a routine inspection."

"Did you find everything in order"?

"We definitely need to add safety tape on the shower floor. This poor kid, uh...."

"Buck"?

Dick snapped his fingers. "Buck, right. Buck took a nasty spill."

Will betrayed no emotion, but inside, he felt suspicious of the man. Buck propped himself up on his elbows to address Will.

"I helped Bear birth a calf. I got covered in O B

Lube. I didn't realize how it would spread when I tried to rinse out. I fell and whacked my head."

Will nodded. Mike was the top dog, but Will was the spiritual leader in the bunkhouse. He wasn't religious. He just had a way of talking to a man's soul and heart.

Dick added, "I brung the kid back to his bunk. His lights were out."

Will didn't care what happened between the two men as long as it was something they both wanted. Judging by the grin on Buck's face and Dick's satisfied smile, it was.

Dick hid his resentment from Will. He felt like the man was always judging him and finding him wanting. Dick was a good boss, a good rancher, and a damn good fuck. He had nothing to hide and felt no shame. Besides, he was Will's boss, so if he didn't like something, Will could just take a walk.

Will wondered why Buck let this man rip him a new one the day after his encounter with Sal. He didn't even know yet about Bear and his colon-twisting invasion. It seemed like maybe the boy had a problem, the same problem that changed girls into fallen women. Will didn't have a name for it, but it was real enough. It was something broken inside.

Buck saw trouble pass across Will's face. Will was disappointed in him. Buck wasn't sure why, so he didn't know how to fix it.

Dick excused himself and headed out to the barn. After the screen door banged shut, Will looked at Buck, his face betraying no emotion.

"Will, what's wrong"? Buck asked.

"I was hoping maybe you could tell me, son."

Buck shrugged. I'm happier than a hog in shit, Will. I had so much sex today, and the sun hasn't set! D and me blew each other. I fucked one ass and got ass-fucked twice today.

"Dick fucked you twice?"

"No, Bear fucked me once, then Dick."

Will whistled. "Can you walk"?

Buck laughed. "Sure!"

"Why don't you get dressed, and we'll go for a walk before dinner."

Buck winced as he got to his feet. He couldn't see it, but a slimy dribble of blood, lube, and semen was steadily leaking from his hole. Will got a washcloth and cleaned the boy gently. His legs were trembling. Will could see the boy was in pain.

The stream of sex juices slowed and came to a stop. Will ran the washcloth softly on Buck's balls and cock, then gave his ass a final wipe.

"Okay, get dressed."

"Yes, sir."

Will frowned. It must be the military that causes him to respond like that.

Buck had to bend at the waist to pull on his jeans, putting pressure on his innards. He cried out despite himself.

"Son, you are sweatin' like a whore in church. You want aspirin?"

Buck nodded and breathed a sigh of relief as he got his jeans past his knees and could straighten up. Will returned with two aspirin and a can of beer to wash it down.

"Whiskey would be best, but we don't have any right now." Will apologized.

Buck gratefully accepted the makeshift balm. He tore the top off the beer and chugged it, washing down the aspirin. He tossed the empty can into a nearby wastebasket. The alcohol did little to numb the pain, but it put Buck in good spirits, which helped.

They headed to the back door. Behind them, they heard Bear enter and turn on the ceiling fan.

"What the fuck!" Bear bellowed, face full of a splattering of Buck's warm cum from the ceiling fan.

Will and Buck walked out the back of the bunkhouse onto a trail that followed the valley's slope, then ran alongside the river. Buck limped a little but was able to keep up with Will's slow, leisurely pace.

Will passed Buck a Marlboro; they puffed as they walked together in silence.

"Will, are you mad at me"?

"Not mad, son, just worried."

"Worried"? Buck was puzzled.

"You overdid things these past couple of days. You're in pain."

Buck bristled. "I'm a man fucker. I can take a man, suck a man, fuck a man...it's my purpose here on Earth. I'm proud of what I do!"

Will nodded. He understood where the boy was coming from. Buck had just found himself sexually. Men were the lucky recipients of his talents, which he gave freely. Perhaps a little too freely, but that was not for Will to decide.

"You know, now beer-can Dick Burns is gonna find an excuse to come around here every day and fuck you." Will figured it was best to be blunt.

"Really"? Will expected fear in the boy's voice, but it was greedy, eager anticipation instead.

"Are you going to be ready for him tomorrow"?

Buck shrugged. "I was in a barracks with a hundred men. That got difficult, but only because everyone was fighting over me. Just six men and one boss feels like a vacation."

Will felt pangs of sadness for Buck. He wondered how far back his story went. Buck was happy to volunteer.

"We had a good life. I loved my Ma and my Pa. We was in Kentucky in a coal mining town. There were jobs a-plenty for men of all ages. My Pa would come home each night with a big smile and a hug for me. Then one day, he didn't come home. Ma thought maybe he had an accident, but he didn't. He fell in love with a girl and left us."

Will listened closely.

"And Ma, she didn't get no benefits, and jobs for women went to the wives whose husbands got kilt in an accident. Weren't no work for victims of adultery."

Will knew where this was going.

"So she did what women do, sometimes. She was pretty and clean, so she was real popular with all manner of men. And she was willing to do all the stuff they asked for.

"Money was good, but one day the welfare folks just showed up and took me to a farm. I never seen my Ma again. I was a prisoner at an orphan farm, with both my parents still alive! I wasn't always on my best behavior, so they sent me to reform school in tenth grade. The minute I turned eighteen, I left and joined the Army."

Will asked, "Is that where you picked up your...skills"?

"The Army, yeah. Not reform school. Bunch of ugly shitheads."

"I interrupted; go on."

"I got put in a unit that didn't have no religious people. That's really all it takes. If nobody is judging, you'll do what pleases you. And since I spied so much on my Ma when she was with her men, I knew all the facts of life, and some facts that hardly nobody in that unit knew."

Will cursed himself for becoming aroused at this story. Hopefully, Buck wouldn't notice.

"So one night, this one big guy came right up to me and told me what he was gonna do to me. So I called his bluff; I took him into the bushes, bent right over, and let him slip his little dick in. A group of guys caught us, but they just wanted their turn. Most of the guys were just regular size. But one soldier they called Billy -- short for Billy club; he was big as a horse."

Will adjusted his hard cock in his pants. He thought he saw Buck catch a sideways glance, but he couldn't be sure.

"When I finally learned how to get Billy all the way down my throat, they cheered. But then he wanted to fuck me. I hadn't been with anyone near that big before."

Will asked, "Was he bigger than Sal or Bear"?

Buck thought for a moment. "Different type, but close. Anyways, so it turns out Billy is an expert on his 'condition' and knows how to break in a new soldier. He had pomade to slick up his shaft, and he went really, really slow. That's how he taught me about the second room, you know, for the big boys."

Will was absentmindedly playing pocket pool, aroused by this boy's unusual past.

"Second room?"

"Well, that's what he called it. That place where the extra long ones go."

"Never been there."

"Me neither, but I've let more than a few guys like Billy into mine."

"Right, keep going."

"He fucked me nonstop for an hour while the guys cheered him on. After that, so long as I let soldiers fuck me every night, it never really hurt. One time I was sick in the infirmary and didn't get with nobody for a week. I near screamed like a virgin when I started up again. It takes constant practice."

Will was astonished by this boy's knowledge.

"Anyways, our little group was growing. I was one of just a few men strong enough to take a hard cock in me, and I was the only one that liked it. Everyone else in the group had to wait their turn to stick it in. Some nights I think I must have had thirty cocks in me. They was lined up in the dark by my bunk."

Will was ashamed that this story turned him on.

"Then the fights started over who was first. It didn't take long for the CO to figure out what them fights was about. The CO was a pain in every way. His dick was big; he had all kinds of perversions. He made me his slave and wouldn't let no one touch me. I missed all my friends. I made them all so happy, and the CO took me away all to his self. He was brutal. I can take all kinds, but if they punch you and spit on you and poke you up inside with things, it ain't right.

"So I got word to Billy that if he ratted out the CO, I would deny ever having been with any of 'em. My buddies knew I was a man of my word, so they sent the Major into the CO's office while he had me tied up and gagged, naked. And I did as I promised. Nobody got in trouble. Not even the CO. He said I tried to rape him, and he had just got me subdued, it just wasn't what it looked like, and they let him stay.

"And that's how I left the Army."

Buck turned, put one hand on Will's crotch, and kissed him right on the mouth. Will wanted to protest, but weeks of pent-up frustration were too strong to fight. He was the oldest cowboy in the bunkhouse. He didn't get much action. Sometimes D would toss him a pity fuck, or Mike would give him a handjob. He knew that Buck was willing...no...wanted to give Will more.

Buck sat on a granite table rock that formed a bench. Buck undid Will's belt and unbuttoned his jeans. His mature cock sprang to attention. It was on the large side of average and perfectly proportioned. His foreskin was a little tight, but Buck slid it back behind the head.

Will did not intend things to go this way. He fought with himself, all the while letting Buck engulf his cock completely with his mouth. Will felt a beautiful sensation as his cockhead slipped past the epiglottis. This was too good. He gave up the fight.

Buck felt safe and relaxed with Will. He had an easy penis, the kind he loved. It was not gonna be cruel or brutal, and it would take no time to accommodate like the gut bruisers back at the bunkhouse. It would never need to visit the second room. Buck worked his perfect meat lovingly, with joy and relief. This man was the age his father must be. Maybe that was why he saved him for last.

Will was careful not to choke the boy, encouraging him to take breaths as he needed to, which, it just so happened, was not often. He felt Buck caress his butt cheeks, and he came to a decision. This boy deserved to fuck Will. The thought of it turned him on. The son fucks his father. It aroused him; it gave him the courage to thrust a little harder, knowing he could pay the boy back for any pain or suffering.

Buck tasted salt. It was the first sign that cum was about to blow. He pulled back, jacking Will's shaft but licking and sucking on the head. Will made grunting noises. He ran his fingers through Buck's hair and said, "Yes, son. Yes, son. I'm gonna come. I'm gonna- oh! I'm coming"!

Buck tasted the first spray of cum across his tongue. He pulled out Will's cock to watch it shoot. It covered his face with weeks of stored sperm. Will cried out with joy. He shot on the young cowboy's chest and arms, painting him with his pearly man juice. Will pointed his cock downwards into his cupped palm and filled it. He held it where Buck could see it. Buck leaned forward to lap it up, but Will shook his head and held it out of reach. Buck's look of dismay turned to one of joy when he saw what Will was using it for. Will carefully applied his semen to his asshole, working some in with one finger.

Buck stood. Will took the remainder of the cum

and rubbed it up and down the young man's cock. He grew startled when he felt the wide spot, but it was too late to turn back. He feared he was in for a real ass stretching tonight.

Will bent across the table rock so his ass was level with Buck's odd-shaped meat. Buck spit a few times, mixing his saliva liberally with Will's come. It wasn't O B Lube, but it was very effective.

Buck entered the first three inches doggy style, knowing right when to stop. Will wiggled his hips in anticipation. "Fuck me, son."

Those words had a dizzying effect on Buck, who wanted so badly to be a good boy for his father once more. If this is what Pa wants, then this is what Buck would give him.

Buck slapped Will on the left buttock sharply. It startled Will, which caused his sphincter to relax for an instant. Buck seized the window of opportunity to make another half-inch of progress. He couldn't be greedy, or there would be blood.

Will buried his face in his jacket sleeve and bit down hard. He had been with Sal and Bear but never got this far. They left him alone because of it. Will didn't know that a segment of Buck's cock was wider than Sal's, wider than Bear's. He hadn't measured. So he wasn't as afraid as he should be. But Buck knew his own body well and knew how to break in a new stallion.

Using gravity to assist him, Buck leaned gently into Will. In fractions of an inch, he was making progress. He paused, even backed up an inch before returning to the depth that Will could tolerate.

Will felt no pleasure. Buck gave him white hot searing pain that blinded him. He cried softly as more and more of Buck's flesh football went inside him. He pounded the rock with his fist, then reassured Buck with lies, "Son, keep going! It feels so fucking good!"

With these words, Buck forced himself past the

wide point so that Will's hole inhaled the rest and clamped down on the narrow base of his cock. With those words, the lies became truth. Will felt relief and a rush of narcotic pleasure following the deep, ripping pain moments earlier.

Buck knew this was the hard part. He had to pull out again and re-enter fully to accustom Will to the wide spot. If he put it off, it would be more painful, so in a single pendulum motion, he swung his hips away until his head nearly popped out and then plunged immediately back in.

Will felt himself being shot in the ass twice in rapid succession. It was the worst pain but led to the greatest pleasure, and now it was happening again. Buck fired up the locomotive and just kept assaulting Will's ass with his cruel instrument of pleasure.

It was perhaps another two minutes, and Buck had thrust at least 25 times before Will realized he was no longer in any pain. His body's natural painkillers had assisted, but so had Buck with his persistent in-and-out assault.

Will unclenched his hands and released his teeth from his jacket. Buck continued to slide in and out of Will, but easily, with no resistance. Will was lifted to new heights of euphoria. He'd never had a son, but if he had, it would have been Buck. Giving this gift to a son was something every father should do for his adult son. It teaches the son how to experience pleasure in a way that pleasures another. It's one of nature's few acts that benefits both parties. And it even teaches the son how to be a better lover to women if the son lets the father have his turn.

"That's right, son! Fuck your daddy!"

Buck heard this, and it sent him dangerously close to the precipice. He slowed and breathed. Will wiggled his hips, begging for more.

Buck wiped the sweat from his brow and continued

his excavation of Will's insides. The man lying before him on the rock made Buck miss his Pa. He'd lost all contact and had been searching for him in every man since. Will was the closest to a father he had met since joining the Army. His CO was an asshole. The true father figures, Majors and Colonels, were beyond his reach. But here at the bunkhouse, he found Will, who cared for him like a son but fucked like a lover.

Buck began to take his whole cock out of Will, stroke it a few times, then plunge it back in to the hilt. This gave him a view up inside Will as the gaping hole closed slowly. Buck would wait until it had almost snapped shut before entering again.

Will moaned with new delight at the change in technique. Buck was giving him a pleasure he had never known. It was the electric bond of their fatherly friendship, combined with the feeling of the night air blowing gently inside his gaping ass between strokes...it was causing him to build to a climax.

Buck rolled Will onto his back so he could see his face. He grabbed hold of Will's ankles to steady himself while thrusting in this new position. The change increased the pressure on Will's prostate, causing clear seminal fluid to dribble from his stiff dick. Buck let go of Will's ankles and used the rock to support his weight. This brought him very close to Will. Will's dick drooled on Buck's abdomen and his own. Buck looked into Will's paternal eyes as their faces drew closer. Then, like a pair of magnets, they suddenly locked lips. Buck had kissed plenty of men, but he had never kissed a man like Will. He hungered for his kind, gentle protection. They explored each other's tongues while Buck penetrated Will; this created a bond as tight as solder, holding them together as one.

This oneness, this sensation of two souls uniting through love and sex, this was what Buck had been searching for. He found sex in the Army and more sex in the bunkhouse, but here, under the Montana night sky, he finally found love.

Will had always wanted a young man like Buck to share his sleeping bag. He wanted to coach and guide the boy. He wanted to teach him how to love and be loved in return. He wanted his tongue and his ungodly thick cock inside him, too. It was all connected. As each second passed, the kiss intensified. Will put his arms around Buck, wrapped his legs around Buck's waist, and held him closer. Buck felt a brand new sensation that he couldn't describe or name. It was a current of energy that was intertwined with lust and love. It didn't start in his balls. It began in his heart and radiated to all parts of his body. It felt like every part of him was going to come. He looked at Will, who nodded and said, "I feel it too."

Everywhere Buck's flesh touched Will's, there was the same tingling he felt in his dick right before he shot a load. It was all over his body. Buck quaked with desire, spreading his trembling to Will, who vibrated with the same intense current. Buck breathed heavily, sweat dripping onto his partner from his brow. He threw back his head and shouted, "Oh Shit! Holy shit!"

And as if it were the first time in a week, Buck felt his balls let loose a torrent of milky white fluid. It made Buck cry.

Buck's ejaculation hit Will's rectum walls so hard that he gasped aloud. More and more hot man butter basted his asshole; his own semen that they'd used as lube merged with the young man's effluence forming a male bond like no other. It put Will over the edge, and he sprayed a load between their bellies without even touching himself.

Buck held Will in a mutual embrace, his head resting on the older man's right shoulder so he wouldn't see the tears. They remained locked and vibrant for several minutes until Buck grew soft and slid out of Will on a flash flood of expelled semen.

The two men lay on their backs, breathing. Buck dried his eyes with his forearm. Will smiled at the new recruit.

"Tears of joy"?

Buck was embarrassed. "Tears of relief."

"Relief from what"?

Buck's heart was pounding now. He was vulnerable. Did he dare express his heart's desire to this man he'd only just met? Was that his imagination earlier, or had something transcendent taken place between them? The relief of finally feeling loved...

"I ain't sure."

Will laughed. "Let me make it easy for you. I felt it; it was real, and I hope you feel what I feel now."

Buck smiled. "Yep. I do feel it."

Will was pleased that his new friend was honest with him. "Son, I hope we can make it a real thing."

"But Will, the other guys are gonna want more tail. Like you said, Dick Burns will be sniffing around every day. Bear, Mike, Sal...they all want me."

"What do you want, son"?

Buck grew quiet. He was ashamed of the desires that seemed to conflict with one another. He wanted the love and protection of a father figure like Will. He wanted to be with Will. But he needed to share his gifts with all the men. It wasn't a mere desire but a necessity, like food or water. How could he love a man so completely and yet allow himself to serve the needs of any man who happens along?

"I am not sure what your silence means, Buck, so let me see if I can help."

"I'm confused."

"I know, son. Sex and love are tricky partners. The Bible tells other folks to be faithful to one another. And look how many wars and murders we got."

Buck laughed, "Amen."

"You told me your story about how you found your purpose in life, giving pleasure to men. It's your mission in life. Hell, in a big city, you could make a fortune at it instead of giving it away for free out here in the wilderness."

Buck laughed, "What do you mean"?

"Well, it's not my actual point. See, if I met a painter who painted pictures that brought more joy into the world, and say we was in love, I wouldn't ask him to paint only pictures of me."

Buck understood.

"So, Will, you'd be mine, and I'd be yours, but you'd let me, uh, see other men"?

"I would. I might not always like it, but I sure would love to say you was mine."

"Is this love"? Buck was bewildered.

"I don't know. Why don't you try kissing me and then answer"?

The moon beat down in the Big Hole River Valley, where the Great Plains meet the Continental Divide. Its moonbeams landed on an older cowboy and a green-horn, lips locked, pawing at one another with renewed desire. It wasn't the first time the moon had seen such love, and it was not the last. But true love takes many shapes, and no matter how odd, so long as it is true, that love receives the moon's blessing. A young man searching for a father and an old cowboy looking for a son found each other that night. And the moon con-tinues to shine on them for always.

ABOUT PETER SCHUTES

Peter Schutes is a fictional character. He was modeled after the gay pulp fiction authors of the 1970s and 1980s. His creator often wondered who the men were who wrote these books, and so he created Peter to satisfy his curiosity.

Peter was born in 1896 to a wealthy New England family. His whole life, he carried a massive burden: he had a gigantic penis. His sex life was defined by the men who worshipped him.

Peter led a tempestuous life, which is documented in the fictional masterpiece "The Autobiography of Peter Schutes." To learn more about this prolific and prodigious author, we recommend reading his immortal tale of life with too much of a good thing.

OTHER BOOKS FROM PETER SCHUTES PUBLISHING

E-books and Paperbacks (as noted)

The Able Seaman

The Anaconda Copper

The Autobiography of Peter Schutes*

Backwoods Delivery

Big Bodies of All Sizes*

Bobbing Buoys and Salty Seamen*

Bunkhouse Buddies*

The Butt Baby*

Cloistered

Confessions of a Rodeo Clown*

Dark as a Dungeon*

Demonic Deception *aka* Deceived, Cursed & Blessed

Desert Island Daddies

The Expectant Member

Firehouse Lovers

The Fish

Five Erotic Tales*

The Gospel of Priapus*

Hercules and Lippos

Hobo Honey

Hot Blue Collars*

Hotshot

Logger's Delight

Muscle Bottom*

Panama Heat

Satanic Seductions*

Satan's Sissy Boy

The Slaves of Rome*

The Thigh Baby

Under the Boardwalk

World's Biggest

Coming Soon

Backwoods Delivery - The Complete Daddy's Boy Series

Like the Greeks Do*

Higher Education*

Hoboes, Hustlers, and Jailbirds*

Small Cockpits and Big Hangars*

Tales of Two Daddies*

*Available as Paperbacks

www.ingramcontent.com/pod-product-compliance
Lightning Source LLC
Chambersburg PA
CBHW011143310726
48972CB00009B/2827